"W... ...ing about?"
Stephen asked gently.

"Senator, I'm going to take the 'Fifth' on that one, if you don't mind!"

Katharine looked away, a smile breaking on her lips. "Let me say I'm not thinking very rationally at the moment. I can't be held responsible for my thoughts!"

"Well, I can and I think right now we should get of this car and walk for a while." He kissed her and held her close, then said breathlessly, "For a man who always has to control his feelings and represent his constituents in a calm, rational way, all I can say is—I'm glad I don't have to be speaking in the Senate at this hour!"

They got out of the car and began to walk along the river, Stephen's arm tightly around her shoulders. Katharine felt that this was the most perfect night of her life...

Joan Winmill Brown, who first gained recognition as an English actress, has most recently received plaudits for her skill as an editor and compiler of Christian anthologies. Her reading audience will be delighted with her most recent work in the area of Christian romance novels as she writes from her interesting background.

If Love Be Ours

JOAN WINMILL BROWN

HARVEST HOUSE PUBLISHERS, INC.
Eugene, Oregon 97402

Other Rhapsody Romance Books:

The Heart That Lingers
Another Love *(Coming Fall 1989)*
With All My Heart *(Coming Fall 1989)*

IF LOVE BE OURS

If Love Be Ours

Chapter One

The door to the narrow, eighteenth-century Georgetown row house closed quietly. Katharine Hayes leaned her sleek blonde head against its comforting presence and sighed. The day had been grueling. Washington, D.C., was in the grip of an oppressive heat wave, but now the cool, welcoming hallway of her small rented house allowed her the luxury of being able to unwind. Armed with a mass of books and files that were her "homework" for tomorrow's TV interviews, she kicked off her shoes and made her way down the two steps leading to the kitchen.

Katharine dumped the books and files onto the kitchen table and went immediately to the refrigerator and poured herself a long, cool drink. She looked in the freezer, but nothing tempted her. Perhaps later.

Walking back to the living room, deep in thought, she turned on the lamp by the piano and sat down on the old rosewood stool. Katha-

rine had furnished the house with several antiques which she had brought with her from the
family home in Connecticut, and they harmo-
nized completely with their eighteenth-century
setting.

She continued to sip her cool drink and remembered all that had transpired during the
day. From the time she had awakened she had
known it would be hectic. Three investigative
interviews—one with a congressman up at the
Hill—then she had subbed over at the White
House at the President's news conference. He had
actually called her by her first name. She smiled
at the thought of having been called "Katharine"
by the President of the United States!

Softly at first, she began to play a theme from
Paganini. But as she relaxed the notes poured
forth, almost in a torrent, releasing the pent-up
emotions she always felt after the late-night
newscast at the television studio.

More and more she found that music calmed
her, helping her to see more clearly the important factors of her life. In Washington it was easy
to become so involved in the social and political
whirl that surrounded her, plus the ambitious
drive that kept her straining to achieve the
ultimate, as far as she was concerned...
anchorwoman.

Katharine had attained that position in her

home state of Connecticut, after apprenticing first as a spot announcer, then graduating to investigative reporting. The news director from WNSC in Washington, D.C., had seen her and asked her to come to the capital as an investigative reporter—with the promise that it could possibly lead to anchorwoman. That had been six months before. Even though Katharine had been praised for her work, Sally Denton, who had been with the station for several years, was safely entrenched and had a large following of viewers. Katharine had now been told it would probably be some time before a vacancy would arise. In the meantime, she was happy to get as much experience as possible. National anchorwoman was her goal and at twenty-eight she felt she still had a few years to achieve it.

Continuing to play, Katharine smiled as she looked at her sister's photograph on the piano. Surrounded by her family, Ellen looked serene and completely happy. She had married Jim Bartlett nine years before, when he was a lieutenant in the Army—now he was a colonel and stationed at the Pentagon, where he held an extremely sensitive and important position. They had moved to Bethesda and Katharine would often drive over to see them. It was a haven for her. They seemed to be entirely content, even though Jim worked long hours and was often out of town on classified work.

Ellen had always been the domesticated child in the family. Katharine, on the other hand, invariably had her nose in a book or in the latest newspaper. Pausing to look around her living room, she wished she had inherited Ellen's talent for making a house look like a welcoming home. She planned to ask Ellen to come over some time and help her decorate this quaint old, creaky house. Katharine had masses of ideas and good intentions, but she never quite found the time to carry them out.

Ellen's children, Jamie, aged seven years, and five-year-old Beth, were typical American children —fun-loving, mischievous and both were great favorites of their Aunt Katharine. She thought that perhaps this weekend she would find time to drive out to Bethesda and take them to the zoo. They were crazy about animals and Jamie reminded Katharine of herself when she was young. He was always asking questions, sometimes rather leading ones that demanded a complete answer about the procreation of certain animals.

Katharine gazed wistfully at Jamie's bright young face in the photograph. Had she perhaps given up too much for her career? There had been opportunities to settle down, but she knew she could never make any man happy until this determined, ambitious drive within her had been satisfied.

She went back to playing the piano, now humming the melody as she reflected on her life.

A knock at the front door made her stop her reverie. She glanced at her watch. It was after midnight. Who could possibly be at her door at this late hour? Cautiously, she tiptoed out into the hallway and peered through the peephole in the front door. Katharine could not believe it . . . Stephen Douglass, America's youngest senator, was standing on her doorstep. They had met the previous week, when she had interviewed him at the Capitol and he had driven her home when the camera crew had received a call to go to another story.

Hastily she looked in the mirror, making sure that her mascara had not smudged around her large expressive blue eyes. She ran her hands through her blonde hair and straightened the collar of her pale pink dress as the Senator knocked on the door once more. Katharine opened it and hesitated for a moment.

"Hi!" Stephen's dark-haired, dynamic good looks seemed to light up her doorstep. He was known for his captivating smile, which disarmed many of his would-be political enemies as it was now disarming her.

"Well, hi," Katharine said, rather shyly.

"I was just taking Blarney for his nightly run and heard the piano. You have many talents, Katharine."

"Well, thank you." She had not even noticed Stephen's Irish setter at his heels. "Please, do come in." Then, remembering she had not straightened the living room, she added, "You'll have to excuse the chaos. I never seem to have time..."

"You don't mind the dog?" Stephen asked, completely ignoring her excuses.

"Of course not. I miss our family dog so much."

Blarney shot through the entrance and made his way down the steps to the kitchen.

"He seems to know where the food is," Katharine laughed. "Perhaps you would like a cup of coffee?"

"Sounds great. I am so bushed, but I was wound up after an excruciating debate in the Senate today. I knew I could never get to sleep, and then Blarney reminded me I hadn't taken him for his evening run."

Stephen Douglass lived only three streets away in a house that was almost a copy of Katharine's, but at least three times as large. "The English seemed to have been in a rut when it came to floor plans in the eighteenth century," he laughed, looking around the charming house.

"Yes, but I really adore these old houses, don't you?"

Stephen nodded. "There's such a feeling of permanence about them. Each day when I come home from the Hill I am reminded that no matter how frustrating the day has been, the house has endured through years and years of political storms and yet it continues to remain standing."

Katharine nodded as they entered the kitchen and she went to make the coffee. "Those are my sentiments entirely. Somehow there is a peace about this place that envelops me when I open the front door."

Stephen peered out of the kitchen window and saw the small but charming walled garden with its large shade trees.

"I see you have a delightful retreat outside, too."

"Why don't we sit out there and have our coffee?" Katharine suggested. "Blarney might enjoy it much better than being cooped up in the house." He had been sitting by the back door, looking pleadingly at her and when she opened it he bounded out into the garden.

"It looks as if you have quite a mountain of work ahead of you," Stephen said, gesturing toward the pile of books and files on the kitchen table.

Katharine had forgotten them and was immediately brought back to the reality of tomorrow. "Oh dear, that reminds me. . .I will have to turn you out after we've had coffee. I do have a great deal of information to sort through before tomorrow's interviews," she said apologetically.

"Blarney and I will be on our way in a very short time, I promise you."

"I'm being very remiss, Stephen. Would you care for something to eat?" Katharine was trying not to appear flustered around this remarkably attractive man. When he declined, she gave an almost inaudible sigh of relief. There was nothing exciting in the refrigerator. She found some cookies that did not look too stale and took the tin with her out to the garden. Stephen followed with the coffee.

It was a bright moonlit night and as they sat under the large oak tree on the white wrought iron chairs, Stephen put his feet up on the matching table and sighed.

"Peace, utter peace. Sometimes I think all of us in Congress are going mad. Everyone loves the sound of his or her voice. I am possibly the most guilty," he said with a grin.

Katharine smiled. Stephen Douglass, a junior senator from Virginia, was known for his long impassioned speeches. His victorious election campaign had been widely reported. At thirty-one, not only was he America's youngest senator, he was fast proving himself to be the most eloquent also. Older, more seasoned senators had been forced to admit that Douglass was someone to be reckoned with. It was often conjectured that he would no doubt be presidential material in the years ahead. Born into an old established political family, he had inherited the Douglass' good looks and compelling personality.

When Katharine had interviewed him the previous week, she had been struck by his penetrating hazel eyes. They made her almost forget her carefully prepared questions. Though they were written down on a clipboard, she had lost her place. She knew that *he* knew he was having quite an effect on her! Now, sitting with him in her garden, she felt a little more at ease, but still very much aware of his virile presence.

"Katharine, this is excellent coffee, but I'm going to have to bring my own snacks when I call on you again!"

It was impossible for Katharine to be offended —his charm cut right through what would have been another person's insulting remark.

She put her head back and laughed. "I would apologize but quite frankly I have tried to ban anything in the house that might tempt me. The camera adds about ten pounds to a person's image, so the only way I can have any willpower is to just not have anything delicious around."

"Your image looks fantastic to me. In fact, Miss Hayes, you are a very alluring media person. Not quite the cool, assured image I see on the screen, but a warm, exciting woman." He looked into her eyes and there were a few moments of silence that were electrifying.

Katharine knew by his look that he found her exceedingly attractive. "Well, thank you, Senator," she said, slightly embarrassed.

"Katharine, I can't begin to describe how much I enjoyed meeting you last week. You know, I have been interviewed scores of times—but it was so refreshing to talk with you. I knew there was some dimension that the others did not have. Then when you expressed your Christian beliefs it was like a breath of fresh air for me."

"It was for me, too. Sometimes it's rather an uphill battle, but of course we don't have to face it alone. I'm very conscious that He is with me." Katharine smiled at this man she felt close to because of their mutual convictions.

Finishing the last of his coffee, Stephen realized the time and jumped to his feet. "Blarney, we must go and let this beautiful young woman prepare for tomorrow's interviews. Never let it be said we were the cause of her not being able to deliver her usual excellent reports."

Blarney ran ahead of Stephen and waited by the back door. "He's at home already," Stephen commented and as they walked back into the house he put his arm around Katharine's shoulder. She felt a glow go right through her.

Stephen put their cups and saucers in the sink and rinsed them out. "See how domesticated I am?"

Imagining how many servants the Douglass family must have, Katharine thought about how helpful he was. She wondered who had taught him to be so considerate.

"You may be wondering where I picked up this trait, Miss Hayes. I had a governess named Miss Hatfield who insisted that I be thoughtful of others. The years under her care stood me in good stead, bless her. 'Hattie' never let me forget I had a privileged childhood."

"It shows in your concern for others, Stephen. I imagine she is very proud of you."

"Thank you. I hope I never let her down."

Katharine surmised that the governess must have taken over much of his mother's role. Mrs. Douglass was known to be an aloof, matriarchal figure who had ruled the family estate with an iron hand. Since her husband had died, she had earned the reputation of being a very shrewd handler of the Douglass fortune.

Katharine's parents were quite the opposite. Her mother had lived for her family and had always left it to her husband to run the family finances. Katharine adored them both, perhaps putting her father on a slightly taller pedestal.

"May we have dinner tomorrow night, Katharine?"

Stephen's voice brought her thoughts back and she answered quickly, "I would love that. You know my hours, however. It would either have to be very late—a midnight snack—or perhaps on the weekend."

"How about both?" He looked down at her and flashed that disarming smile.

Katharine nodded. "That sounds fine with me."

"Right, tomorrow night I'll call you at the studio right after the news and confirm the time."

As they reached the front door, Stephen found they had lost Blarney. A clatter from the kitchen made them realize where he was. Stephen called him and he came reluctantly up to the hallway, his tail between his legs but still enjoying the remainder of the cookies.

"At least Blarney isn't as fussy as his master," Katharine commented and gave the dog a hug. "Thanks, Blarney, for finishing them and making me feel not such a hopeless hostess." Continuing to stroke the dog's shiny head, she said wistfully, "Oh, how he makes me miss my dog."

"Couldn't you have brought him to Washington?"

"I didn't think it fair to take him away from my mother or his old haunts. My parents often take him to the beach where we have a summer home. He loves to run and explore there."

As Stephen was about to open the front door, he turned to Katharine and said, "Could I ask a favor?"

"Of course."

"Would you play that theme from Paganini once more? I promise to leave immediately. To be truthful, I have heard you play on other nights and listened outside the window, but tonight I decided to knock on your front door."

Katharine thought of him standing in the street listening and she said softly, "You should have let me know before this that you enjoyed Paganini."

Stephen said in a low voice, "That should be 'Paganini as played by Katharine Hayes.' " He reached out and touched her cheek and Katharine felt that same glow go through her once again. She walked toward the piano and quietly began to play the sadly beautiful music. As Stephen sat back and listened, she was conscious that his eyes were upon her.

Blarney came and laid down beside the piano stool. The scene was one of complete serenity, only to be interrupted by the telephone ringing.

Katharine walked over to the side table next to where Stephen sat and picked up the telephone. He started to get up, but she signaled with her eyes for him to stay seated.

"Hello?"

Katharine heard her mother's distraught voice.

"Whatever is the matter, Mother?"

Stephen saw a horrified look come over Katharine's face.

"I don't understand, Mother. How *can* you?"

After listening to a lengthy explanation, Katharine said quietly, "I'll fly up after work on Friday night and we'll talk about it then."

With a few more words of admonition and concern, she put down the telephone and stood there completely dazed by their conversation.

Stephen got to his feet and asked, "Katharine, it's bad news, isn't it?"

"Yes," she whispered, obviously in shock. "My mother is filing for divorce. I just can't believe it. After all these years...I always thought they were the happiest couple. I thought they adored one another..."

She walked over to the fireplace and looking down she said softly, "My mother said that Dad is having an affair with a young woman and all our friends know about it." Tears began to form and she felt embarrassed to let Stephen see her.

He walked over to her and put his arms around her. She looked up at him and he could see the pain in her eyes.

"My governess always used to say, 'Nothing is completely hopeless. We can always pray and let God work out the heartaches.' I have found that to be true many times in my own life, Katharine."

Stephen's words of comfort helped absorb the shattering news she had just received. Wiping the tears from her eyes, she said, "I know, Stephen. God does answer our prayers. It's just such a tremendous shock. I worshiped my father."

"Even someone as beloved to you as your father can have very human failings, Katharine. None of us is infallible. That characteristic was left to our Lord alone."

"That's true," she said and managed a faint smile.

"Would you like me to stay a little longer?" Stephen asked, solicitously.

Katharine shook her head. "I'll be fine, thank you." As she walked to the front door with him, she said, "I'm sorry you had to be drawn into a family problem. Paganini was supposed to have helped soothe your tumultuous day."

"Perhaps just being with you has helped me get my perspective once more." He took her hand and squeezed it. "Try not to worry, Katharine. God is going to work it out."

"Thank you." Katharine bit her lip, then said, "I'm so glad you finally knocked on the door tonight."

"So am I. See you tomorrow night and thank you for a very special interlude. I could listen to you play for hours."

He bent down and kissed her forehead, as she said, softly, "I'll have to give you a concert one day."

"I would like that," Stephen said, looking directly into her eyes. The mood was broken as Blarney bounded down the front doorsteps and Stephen had to chase after him. Stephen turned to wave to Katharine.

As she shut the front door, her mixed emotions caused the tears to flow. So much had happened this evening. Stephen's surprise visit had made her happy with his attention—then the telephone call that had shattered her illusions about her father. She thought of Stephen and the tenderness he had shown and she thanked the Lord that he had been there at that moment.

Walking back to the kitchen and her work, Katharine thought of their meeting again the next night. In spite of her tears, she felt a surge of happiness. Stephen Douglass was becoming very special to her and it seemed so right. . . .

Chapter Two

No amount of makeup beneath Katharine's brilliant blue eyes could hide the telltale signs of fatigue when she faced the cameras the next night. She had hardly slept after her mother's telephone call and her day had been equally as hectic as the previous one. Now, as she gave her special report regarding the children of the inner city and their plight during the long hot summer, she determinedly tried to overcome the tensions of the day.

The news director, Alan Holt, commented to the technicians in the sound booth that, "It looks as if our Miss Hayes is partying a little too much these days."

When the news program signed off, Alan took off his headphones and walked out to the soundstage.

"Katharine, may I have a word with you?"

By the tone of his voice, she anticipated trouble. "Of course, Alan," she replied.

"The camera has an eagle eye—you didn't look your best tonight. Why?" he asked her very directly.

"I'm sorry, Alan. Yesterday and today have been particularly hectic."

"Are you saying the work is too much for you?"

"Of course not. It's just . . ." Katharine paused, not knowing how to answer him. "I've had some rather bad news and I'm sorry it shows."

Alan's tone of voice suddenly changed and he became concerned. "Is there anything I can do, Katharine?"

"Not really, thank you. It's something my family will have to work out." She avoided his searching, questioning eyes. Ever since she first came to work at the station she had felt that if she were to give even the slightest hint that she were interested in him, he would be willing to become more than just her boss. Alan was married with three children, but that did not stop him from admiring and pursuing beautiful women.

"Well, let me know if I can help. And, please, try to get some sleep tonight. Your schedule should be lighter tomorrow, barring some unknown disaster, so take care of yourself."

Connie, the production assistant, interrupted their conversation. "Miss Hayes, Senator

Douglass is on the phone for you."

Alan's eyes met Katharine's and he said, sarcastically, "Remember what I said about getting some sleep, won't you?"

As she thanked Connie, Katharine chose to ignore Alan's remark and walked over to the telephone.

"How about meeting me at the '1740' restaurant?" Stephen's voice sounded so welcome. She told him she could be there in half an hour. It was only two streets from her house and was one of her favorite eating places, specializing in French cuisine.

She called out a quick "Good night" to everyone and felt Alan watching her disapprovingly as she walked to the exit.

"Remember, senators have a way with more than words, Katharine."

"I'll remember," she said noncommittally, sensing again that he assumed her fatigue had more to do with Stephen than her family crisis.

Driving over to Georgetown, her mind was full of the day's events. She had received a call from her sister Ellen, who had been as shocked as Katharine about their mother's decision to file for divorce. But Ellen was not as surprised at their father's supposed infidelity.

"Katharine, Mother has been nagging Dad for so long now. Hounding him to become a better

Christian. I feel sort of responsible in a way. The last time we were all together in Connecticut, Mother and I had a long chat. I told her that even though she had always insisted we attend church and had gone through the ritual herself, she never seemed to have shown the joy of her belief—making others want to know our Lord. From then on she just kept nagging Dad, saying he had never been the example he should have been to us." Ellen had sighed and gone on, sadly, "I just know it isn't too late to stop this divorce. Mother's pride has been hurt and I can sympathize. Without the grace of our Lord, I would find it impossible to forgive Jim if he ever went off with someone else..."

Katharine drove through the wide streets of Washington, almost oblivious to the other cars. Her thoughts turned to Alan and the sarcastic innuendos at the studio tonight. A traffic light turned to red and she slammed on her brakes. Two pedestrians crossed in front of her, shaking their heads. She mouthed a "Sorry" and hoped they understood.

"I have got to get a hold of myself," she thought. Dinner with Stephen would help her to relax. She smiled as a feeling of excitement that had started with his telephone call now mounted.

She had worn a navy blue linen suit on the

news program and had quickly added some exotic, colorful, Peruvian jewelry. Driving up to the restaurant, she looked in the rearview mirror to see if her appearance met with her approval. She was still wearing her television makeup, but in the candlelight it would not be noticed.

Stephen was in the foyer waiting and immediately walked forward to greet her, taking both her hands.

"Katharine!" He bent down and whispered, "You're looking lovely."

Their eyes met and Katharine murmured, "Thank you."

"Our table is ready." Stephen put his arm around her shoulder and the maitre d' escorted them through the charming Early American dining room to a corner table at the rear.

"Each time I come here I wonder if it's going to be my last chance. This building is so rickety."

Katharine laughed and agreed. "I hope they restore it before it's too late. I would really miss this place. It's one of the few restaurants that stays open for dinner at this hour."

They both looked around the quaint dining room, whose sagging beams seemed almost ready to shed the responsibility they had carried out so faithfully for over two hundred years. The diamond-paned windows with their floral curtains sparkled in the candlelight, giving a warm, welcoming atmosphere. Flowers were massed in the fireplace, which was not needed on this hot, humid night.

Katharine turned her attention to the menu. "Everything is fantastic here," she said somewhat wistfully. "I only wish French food was not so fattening."

"You'll begin to look like a rail if you don't eat," Stephen said quietly. "I would think with all the running around that you do during the day you could eat anything. I can't believe you have to worry about that great figure of yours."

Katharine raised her eyebrows and smiled. Leaning forward, she whispered confidentially, "Dream on!" Her expression changed as she remembered Alan's remarks to her as she left the studio. "My looks are half the requirements for my job, so I do have to be careful."

Stephen said appreciatively, "You look beautiful, so don't worry."

Still concerned, Katharine told him about Alan's remarks and Stephen said reassuringly, "I saw the program and really didn't notice anything but perfection, but then I am prejudiced where Katharine Hayes is concerned. Your report on the children of the inner city was excellent. Perhaps you and I could work together on it."

"I would love that. They really need some outlet for all their energy. Most of them are so bored, it's no wonder there's so much petty crime amongst them."

The waiter took their order and they sat back, relaxed and happy to be with one another. Katharine knew that it was an unwritten law not to get emotionally involved with people you interviewed. She had interviewed Stephen a full ten days before, so perhaps, she rationalized, it no longer applied? Though conscious that he was very charming, very handsome, and very influential, there was a quality about him that remained unspoiled and it was this that attracted her.

"Here in Washington, you become so used to being courted by the elite, you sometimes lose sight of the needs of the people you are representing," Stephen said thoughtfully. "My constituents in Virginia are, for the most part, hurting very badly. It's frustrating not to be able to bring about some reforms that will help them immediately . . . but I'm working on it, believe me. The wheels of Congress grind far too slowly." He shook his head dejectedly.

"At least you are doing something," Katharine said. "I'm sure all your efforts are going to pay off one of these days."

The waiter brought their hors d'oeuvres and

they were silent for a few moments. Stephen said suddenly, "Katharine, have you never thought of marriage?"

She looked up, somewhat startled by his question. "Why, of course, but I never thought it fair for me to take on the responsibilities of being a wife, when so much of my time is spent on my career. I have so many other goals that I want to achieve first."

"You sound rather like me. I found myself so caught up in law and then being elected to the Senate, that there has been little time to establish lasting relationships. Do you have any regrets, Katharine?"

"You are a very direct person, aren't you?" Katharine said with a smile.

"My lawyer's mind, I suppose."

"Well, yes, in some ways. When I see my sister and her family lives in Bethesda, she seems so happy. I love her two children and sometimes I think how wonderful it would be to have a child of my own."

"Do you come from a large family?"

"No, there are just the two of us. Complete, absolute opposites and we always have been."

"Sounds like my brother and me. Coming from a political family, naturally my parents expected both of us to go into politics, but Rick has always been a rebel. He would much rather be out in California with his music."

"And doing remarkably well, too," Katharine added. "I take it you do not approve of his style?"

"Oh, no, it's not that—I like country music. It's his questionable *lifestyle* that concerns me. I'm a firm believer in not allowing your behavior to have a derogatory effect on someone else," Stephen said thoughtfully. "Does that sound too pompous? I really didn't mean it to be..."

"It might be to some, but I think I understand. I remember being taught about being a 'stumbling block' to others. Often it seemed I was checked when I desperately wanted to do something, but which might hurt a friend or another person."

Stephen looked across at Katharine as the waiter brought their entree and smiled. "For a first dinner date, I must say we are engaged in some rather heavy topics of conversation. I'm sorry." His dark, intense eyes met hers.

"Please don't apologize, Stephen. I'm enjoying our dinner immensely. Perhaps the two of us are rather alike in a way. We do become so wrapped up in our work and the problems of the world that it is hard to find time for light conversation." She smiled at him and once again felt the mutual attraction.

"That can be very important, Katharine. I intend to see to it that you *find* time to enjoy yourself and forget the rigors of being connected with that frantic world of television."

"Well, thank you and I could say the same for you." She brushed the hair back from her eyes, realizing their friendship was advancing rather swiftly. While they were eating, Katharine was conscious of the eyes of other diners upon them. Stephen Douglass' face was highly visible in Washington and, of course, many knew Katharine's from her news program. She hoped that Alan, her news director, would not make a big issue of her friendship with Stephen. She had seen Alan jealous of anchorwoman Sally Denton's male friends and he seemed to delight in making it difficult for her whenever he could. Likewise, Katharine sensed that the days ahead might not be easy for her.

Stephen's voice brought her back to the charming atmosphere of the restaurant. "My brother Rick is coming home for a week or so. He's giving a concert at Constitution Hall and I'm wondering if I could get him to entertain those inner-city kids while he's here . . . if we could line up a suitable place."

Katharine's eyes lit up.

"That sounds wonderful. I know we could find somewhere. In fact, in doing my report I interviewed some kids in front of an empty supermarket that has a huge parking lot. It's in need

of repair, but perhaps we could get it reno-
vated."

"I'll work on it and see what I can come up
with. In the meantime, are you still flying up
to see your mother tomorrow night?" He had
been hesitant to bring up the subject of her
parents' impending divorce.

Katharine nodded. "Yes, and I'm not looking
forward to it. It's going to be a rather difficult
visit." She sighed, thinking of the weekend that
lay ahead of her.

"May I take you to the airport?"

"Oh, I would really appreciate that. Thank
you. I'm catching the 'red eye' to New York and
then renting a car to drive up to Connecticut.
But if anything interferes I'll understand if you
can't take me . . ."

"Unless a major catastrophe hits, I'll plan on
picking you up. I'm planning to spend the weekend with my mother also. She's having fits about
my life in Washington! She's convinced I'm ruining my health by the hours and the company I
keep!"

Katharine looked at him and said quietly,
"And are you?"

"If having dinner with you is considered de-
structive to my health, I can think of no better
way of being destroyed."

They both laughed. Looking at her watch,

Katharine said, "It *is* almost one o'clock, you know. Perhaps we should forgo dessert."

Stephen reluctantly agreed, admitting he did have to be on the Hill early. "A few of us meet each Friday morning for prayer before tackling the problems of our world. I'm very thankful for that special time together—it really helps."

"I wish there were something like that at the studio," she said reflectively, reaching for her handbag.

Stephen took her hand from across the table and held it tightly. "He's with you wherever you are, Katharine. Don't forget." She nodded, her eyes beginning to fill with tears. He continued, "I'm looking forward to spending a great deal of time with you, Katharine."

"I would like that," she said softly. His voice seemed to hold the promise of many wonderful days ahead to be spent together.

As they walked through the restaurant, Katharine noticed the society columnist from the *Washington Times* sitting at a nearby table and their eyes met. Julia Simpson smiled knowingly at Katharine.

Stephen opened the restaurant door for Katharine and they glanced back to see Julia... heading for the telephone.

Chapter Three

Katharine was awakened by the telephone the next morning. Her sister Ellen's voice sounded somewhat disturbed beneath her "Good morning."

Arranging her pillow and sitting up, Katharine tried to awaken, but she had experienced difficulty sleeping and now the morning light shining through the windows and Ellen's bright voice were an unwelcome intrusion.

"Have you see the *Times*?" Ellen asked.

"Ellen, I haven't even seen the morning yet. Whatever is wrong? I do need my beauty sleep, you know."

"Well, I waited as long as I could, but you, my dear sister, are a major item in Julia Simpson's column."

Katharine groaned.

"She says she saw you and Senator Douglass being very cozy over dinner. Holding hands by candlelight, et cetera, et cetera."

"Spare me the rest. I haven't even had coffee yet." Katharine immediately thought of what her news director would say when she got to the studio. Even so, she had to admit that she was thrilled to be linked to Stephen.

Ellen went on—"Do you think it wise to act like that in public, Katharine? After all, you are very visible these days on television."

A sigh escaped Katharine. "Ellen, all he did was touch my hand when he was making some point or other. Julia has blown it all out of proportion."

She promised to call Ellen later and after putting on her robe and slippers, Katharine went downstairs to get the newspaper and make coffee. Turning to Julia Simpson's column she read:

> Acting as if it were a secret rendezvous between two lovers, Senator Douglass and Katharine Hayes of WNSC were seen dining at the "1740" restuarant last night. Holding hands by candlelight...

The telephone rang and it was Stephen. "Hi! How did you enjoy our madly romantic dinner last night?" His voice had a rather delighted tone.

"Oh, Stephen, I'm sorry. I really am."

"I'm not. I didn't realize we were behaving in quite such an obvious manner, but that's fine with me. If Julia Simpson saw us that way, who cares? Actually, she only wrote what I was feeling." He paused for a moment. "Mother has been on the phone and has given me her lecture for the day."

"So has my sister—you would think we were teenagers!"

They both laughed. "I don't think I could ask for a retraction. It would be difficult to prove I'm not enamored by you, Miss Hayes."

Katharine poured herself a cup of coffee and smiled. "I'm glad," she whispered. "But then I'm still not thinking clearly."

"Will you be sorry later, when you are wide awake?"

"No. Only wondering about Alan Holt and his comments. He has a strange way of reacting to his staff's friendships. A few months ago there was quite a lot of publicity about a fellow employee who had fallen in love with someone. He made life extremely difficult for her at work."

"Same circumstances?"

"What do you mean?"

"The part about falling in love with someone?"

"Oh, Stephen." Katharine was taken aback, yet she knew it was not far from the truth.

"Well, I'll let you go, beautiful one, but remember I'm picking you up tonight to take you to the airport."

Katharine thanked him and put down the receiver, charmed by his warm, understanding personality that now seemed to be becoming a part of her life. Catching sight of herself in the small mirror near the kitchen sink, she could see that she was radiating happiness, even though there was still a feeling of uneasiness. Katharine made herself a piece of toast and, looking out of the window, she saw that the hazy summer sun was causing shadows beneath the large oak tree where she had sat with Stephen two nights before. She unbolted the back door and carried her coffee and toast into the already oppressive, sultry air.

Sitting at the table, she remembered how Stephen had stretched out, so relaxed. The days ahead, she hoped, would find him often at her house...

Her thoughts turned to her parents and she felt a chill go through her. They just had to resolve their problems—Katharine could not bear to think of their parting forever.

She put her elbows on the table and bowing her head in her hands, she prayed, "Father, forgive me, I do forget so often that you are really so close to me and that you want me to lean on you at times like these. Please, right at this moment comfort both of them—wherever they are, whatever they are doing..."

The sound of the telephone ringing intrusively into her time of quiet made Katharine reluctantly stand to her feet. Hastily looking around at the flowers in the garden, she made a mental note to water them before leaving for the studio.

Connie, the production assistant, was calling her. "Miss Hayes, Mr. Holt has asked me to tell you that Sally Denton is ill and will not be able to anchor tonight, so he would like you to sub for her. It means you won't have to cover any outside stories today."

Katharine, with mixed emotions, thanked Connie, who said, excitedly, "And if you don't mind my saying, Miss Hayes, I read Julia Simpson's column this morning and well . . . wow!"

Smiling to herself, Katharine wanted to react rather like that too, but she heard herself answer, calmly, "Thank you, Connie, and tell Mr. Holt I will be in early this afternoon."

She ran her hands through her hair, delighted to think she would be anchoring that evening. Immediately she wondered just what she would wear and running upstairs to her bedroom, she flung open her closet door and looked critically through the clothes hanging there. A red cotton Oscar de la Renta suit, that she had bought on sale at Garfinckels, came into view. She had been saving it for a special occasion and this would be perfect!

Her suitcases, stored on the floor of the closet, caught her eye—making her remember she would have to pack before leaving for the studio. Jeans, a bright blue sweater—just in case it was cool on the beach at night in Connecticut—a couple of blouses, and a dress were all she would need.

Folding her clothes into the suitcase, she suddenly thought how uncaring she had been. Sally Denton was ill and all she had thought about was herself. Katharine dialed the studio and asked to speak to Connie again.

"I forgot to ask what's wrong with Sally?"

"Well, the doctor seems to think it could be appendicitis. She's checked in at the Walter Reed Medical Center for some tests, Miss Hayes."

"Thanks, Connie—see you soon."

Katharine dialed a local florist and asked that flowers be sent to Sally, with a card saying, "Praying for you. Get well soon. Love, Katharine."

"I really do mean that, Lord, even though this is a wonderful opportunity for me."

After showering and shampooing her hair, she sat by the dressing table drying and styling it, wondering if she should call Stephen at the Senate office building. He would be delighted for her *and* she knew he would say a prayer for her success.

Maggie, his secretary, answered and when she heard who was calling sounded cool and distant. "Senator Douglass is extremely busy this morning, Miss Hayes. I'll give him the message that you called."

Rather crestfallen, Katharine put down the receiver, but her resilient nature bounced her back immediately. No icy secretary was going to spoil this day for her. She finished dressing and gathering together her suitcase and garment bag, Katharine ran downstairs and made sure that everything was locked. Then she remembered she had not watered the flowers and ran out to the garden and turned on the hose, her thoughts going a mile a minute. There was so much happening today.

The geraniums and azaleas gratefully drank the cool, welcome water. Washington's weather was merciless at this time of year. Before turning off the hose she filled a watering can and ran back into the house and up to the front door. There she watered the bright red geraniums in the urn on the top step and hoped they would survive until she returned on Sunday night.

After making sure that everything was locked up, she was ready to leave. As she waited for a taxi under a tree by the curb, she turned to look up at her quaint townhouse. Situated between two larger homes, it looked as if it had been an afterthought on the part of the builders. Katharine always assumed it had been sandwiched into an existing space, leaving just enough room for a small alleyway leading to her garden at the back of the house. Its red brick and white wooden shutters gave the structure a warm, welcoming appearance. She would be glad to see it again on Sunday night, when she returned from Connecticut.

She hailed a taxi and asked to be taken to the WNSC studio. With great anticipation, she sat watching the ever-changing, exciting Washington scene. The taxi drove past the White House and she momentarily wondered if the President would be watching the news tonight. Her stomach suddenly fluttered and she looked ahead, trying not to think of *who* would be watching but what she had to do to get ready for the evening's program. There would be the news to read through, decisions to be made with Alan regarding which were the most important items to be covered...then typing her script, timing it all, and making sure there would be space for any late-breaking news items.

All Katharine had read in the *Times* that morning was Julia Simpson's column—definitely not a subject she would be mentioning. Now she would have to catch up on all the local and world news.

Katharine paid the taxi driver and then pushed her way through the revolving doors into the studio, heading toward her dressing room. Alan, who met her in the corridor, was very distant, but Katharine smiled at him, saying, "I'll be with you in a few minutes."

Shutting her dressing room door, she tried to compose herself. "Lord, please don't let him get me down today. I must concentrate on this opportunity..."

Katharine unzipped her garment bag and took out the red suit. Noticing it would need to be pressed, she called the wardrobe department. A few minutes later the telephone rang, just as she was leaving the room, and it was Stephen.

"I didn't think you would get my message," she said, feeling very relieved.

"Why?"

"Well, your secretary didn't sound too thrilled when I told her who was calling."

"Don't take any notice of Maggie, she always guards me like a lioness. I'm always telling her that I should be available to my constituents whenever possible."

"I'm not one of your constituents, remember?" Katharine said amusedly.

Stephen laughed. "I know. I didn't call you because I have to—I very much want to..."

The tone of his voice made Katharine almost

forget for a few seconds why she had called him. "I wanted you to know I'll be anchoring tonight, so say a prayer for me," she said excitedly. She explained the circumstances and Stephen promised he would be praying for her and watching the program.

"In fact, I'll probably see it on the monitor in the waiting room, there at the studio."

Katharine said gratefully, "It will be wonderful to know you are so close. . ." There was a pause by both of them, as the full implication of those words took effect.

"I'm delighted for you, Katharine. You'll be superb, I know."

A knock at the door told her it was time to go meet with Alan. During the discussion with her news director, nothing was said about the item in the *Times*, until they needed to come to a decision as to what local news should be covered on their "Washington People" report.

"There's a lot of gossip in the newspaper, but then I wonder if our viewers would think that someone dining with a senator would be newsworthy?"

"I really doubt it," Katharine said lightly. "There must be more interesting and truthful items we could cover."

Alan turned to look at her and said cuttingly, "Are you saying that Julia Simpson was lying about seeing you with Stephen Douglass at the '1740' restaurant last night?"

"No, that was the truth, but as far as it being a secret rendezvous between two lovers, I would say she was very much mistaken."

Katharine walked over to her typewriter and proceeded to type her script for the evening news—interrupted occasionally by fellow members of the news team wishing her well. She was trembling inside, but outwardly she did not betray her feelings. Alan walked away, shouting to Connie to get him some decent coffee and slammed the door to the newsroom.

Connie remarked with resignation, "Ooh, he's in one of his moods today." She smiled at Katharine and winked. "All I can say is . . . wow, Miss Hayes. Senator Douglass is *really* handsome!" She walked over to the coffee machine and said dreamily, "I can't even get a date with a page up at the Hill. . ." Her big brown eyes, which matched her mass of curly brown hair, registered her aspirations.

Pouring a cup of coffee, Connie went in search of Alan—hoping to placate him.

• • •

At 10:55 P.M. Katharine was making last-minute adjustments to her script and praying that she would be able to concentrate. The makeup man came over and hastily powdered her nose, assuring her she looked sensational. Then the floor manager gave her the signal that in just ten seconds she would be on the air.

"Good evening, this is Katharine Hayes, substituting for Sally Denton who is ill this evening. In just a few minutes we will be back with our first story—a late-breaking incident from Israel, as today the Israeli cabinet met in emergency session."

A commercial came on and Katharine settled back more easily in her chair. Her opening statement had gone well and her confidence was returning. She looked up at the control booth and could see Alan giving her a thumbs-up sign, which made her feel even more assured.

The floor manager gave her a signal and she was once more before the viewers. Item after item of news was given with just the right amount of dignity befitting an anchorwoman.

At the end of the program, as she was taking off her microphone, the other members of the news staff congratulated her and even Alan came into the studio applauding.

"Excellent, Katharine, really excellent."

"Well, thank you, Alan," she said relieved and a little amazed at his enthusiasm. "I'm glad I didn't let the news team down."

He came over to her and put his arm around

her shoulder. "Let's go and have a bite to eat and celebrate," he said lightheartedly.

"I'm sorry, I have to go to the airport. I'm flying up to see my parents in Connecticut."

"Then let me take you to the airport." He walked with her to the exit door of the sound stage, with his arm still around her shoulder.

"Thank you, Alan . . . I already have a ride." Katharine knew that the next few minutes would be difficult.

"Who's taking you?"

Katharine looked up at him and said quietly, "Stephen Douglass."

At that moment Stephen came into the corridor and walked toward Katharine—his arms outstretched.

"You were wonderful, Katharine, absolutely wonderful!"

She took his hands and thanked him rather hesitantly, all the while conscious of Alan's reaction. Muttering something about having a good weekend, he turned away and walked into his office—predictably slamming the door.

"That, I take it, was Alan?" Stephen said rather apologetically. "Very bad timing. I'm sorry."

Katharine shrugged her shoulders and sighed. "He will get over it. He just offered to take me to the airport."

"Would you rather that he did?" Stephen

looked down at her, concern in his eyes.

She looked back into his face and said, "What do you think?"

Stephen kissed her briefly on the cheek and whispered, "Let's get out of here!"

Chapter Four

The drive to the airport took Katharine and Stephen past many of Washington's magnificent, floodlit government buildings and monuments. Their imposing structures always impressed her. Although she had worked in the nation's capital for over six months, Katharine never seemed to get over the thrill of living amid the embodiment of America's history. She thought to herself that she would always have the objective view of a tourist. The sophistication of the city had not completely enveloped her and she was glad.

Stephen looked over at Katharine as he drove over the bridge leading to National Airport and smiled. His hand tightened over hers and he said regretfully, "I sure wish I could go with you, Katharine. Just know my thoughts are going to be with you all the time."

She looked down at his hand as it clasped hers. It was so strong, yet it had the capability of making her feel the gentleness and comfort she so needed. Looking over at him she said, "I wish you could, too." She turned to watch the moonlight reflected in the smooth water of the Potomac as it flowed under the bridge. The impressive Jefferson Memorial cast a glorious, peaceful image on the water. Katharine felt rather dejected at leaving the city she had come to consider her second home. Now, having met Stephen, it seemed even more meaningful to her.

All too soon the turnoff to the airport came into view and it was time to leave each other. As Katharine walked to the plane, she still could feel the impact and sensation of Stephen's kiss. It had not been like the others. . . halting on the forehead or cheek. . . but a long, impassioned kiss that told Katharine his feelings for her were becoming like hers—deeper and more fervent.

• • •

The flight to New York was a short one and soon she found herself driving along the turnpike to Connecticut in her rented car. A slight summer shower bathed the windshield, making it difficult to see the road. It was a few minutes before she realized that the wipers needed turning on—her thoughts had been still in Washington and with Stephen. She missed him already, and the loneliness of the drive was increased, knowing he was so many miles away.

Now as familiar landmarks came into view, she began to seriously think again of all there would be to face. Katharine wondered if she would get to see her father. They had lived through so many wonderful times together. The house in Greenwich had always been open to her friends...barbecues, parties. She had felt at ease sitting and talking with her parents about all her hurts, cares, and triumphs.

Driving on, she remembered a day when she had been only twelve years old and she had felt the whole world was caving in on her. Her best friend had proved to be disloyal. Her father had taken her out in the garden and while he pushed her on the swing that he had made for her, he had talked about what life was really all about. There would be plenty of hurts and disappointments, but there would also be times when you knew it was all worthwhile. Hurts were there for "growing." You either learned, accepted, picked yourself up and went on—or you became bitter and resentful and the love inside you was crushed, like a flower that had begun to show its head above the soil and then was suddenly trodden down to slowly die.

"Never let that happen to you, Katharine. Love is the most important part of life. God's love for you can never be crushed or killed. Whatever you will face will be faced in the light of His love, so hang in there, little Katie and you'll never be alone."

Tears came to her eyes as she remembered his tenderness. That day, when her mother had called from the house to say lunch was ready and Father had helped her off the swing, they had run up the hill to the white clapboard house. It had been a warm, loving home because of a mother and father who really loved each other.

"Did I only imagine they were really happy? Were they merely hiding their differences from me?" Katharine tried to remember when they had ever argued. Of course, there were some disagreements over the years, but usually one or the other gave in good-humoredly and they were seemingly soon forgotten.

She remembered being taken to church. The whole family sat together in the same pew each week. Ellen was the model worshiper, in her white gloves and black patent shoes, listening attentively and singing the hymns with all her heart. Katharine smiled to herself as she thought how different she was. "Miss Wriggleworm" her mother and father nicknamed her. No matter how hard she tried, she could never sit still. And when it was time for the children to leave the sanctuary for Sunday school, Katharine was always delighted. It meant a drink of Kool-Aid and a cookie and she would be able to run around for a few minutes. Then when the lesson started she would be the one who would always ask the questions—sometimes embarrassing the young woman who taught them with the profundity of her inquiries. Ellen, who was two years older, would try to catch Katharine's attention, shaking her head and whispering, "Mother says you must try to *listen*, Katie . . . like *me*." Katharine would sometimes give her a good pinch and Ellen would let out a bloodcurdling yell—ruining her image! Katharine laughed out loud at the memory.

Both children always said their parents loved the other child the most: "You always play favorites, Mother. Ellen never gets into trouble. It's always me you blame."

Katharine's mother had taken her in her arms many times and whispered, "Katie, you're so much like I was when I was your age—always getting into mischief. I don't love you less; perhaps I understand you more. When God made mothers He made them with hearts that have room to love each one of their children equally."

The car got closer to Mystic, near where the family summer home was. She began to experience a little tug at her heart that was reminiscent of when as a child she would return from a trip and she would see her mother sitting on the porch that went entirely around the old house by the sea—waiting with a smile on her face to welcome her daughter home.

The rain had stopped and Katharine turned off the windshield wipers. Glancing at the clock in the dashboard, she saw that it was after 2 A.M. She turned the car down the lane that led to their house. Katharine had not seen it for some time and already everything looked different to her. The white, wooden gate with "Gull's Wings" painted on it, was missing one of its hinges and creaked forlornly in the light sea breeze. Several years before they had all made it a project to paint the name of the house on the gate and laughingly Katharine had pronounced it the grandest-looking gate on the lane. Now neglect had transformed it into a sorry looking object, desperately in need of attention.

Katharine drove up the winding overgrown driveway. Overhanging briars brushed past the car, making her feel as if she were entering the domain of some reclusive family—not the happy, close-knit family who had enjoyed so many carefree summers together.

The large oak tree overlapped the roof of the house, almost dwarfing its architecture. Victorian, the residence had a solid, stable feel to it still. Katharine could see herself climbing the great oak tree and venturing onto the roof, with Ellen shrieking, from the safety of the porch, "Be careful, Katie!"

The family dog, Bruno, a now elderly black spaniel, barked at the offending car as Katharine drove up. He watched as she got out and called his name. At first there was no sign of recognition, then his tail began to wag and he leaped toward Katharine, who caught him up in her arms. She was not conscious that her mother had come out onto the porch and was watching the scene of welcome.

"Katie . . ." The soft, gentle voice made Katharine turn toward her.

"Mother!" She ran up the steps and was in her welcoming arms. "How good to see you."

They went into the house, arm in arm, still trying to control all the emotions they were feeling. Katharine noticed her mother seemed to have aged ten years. The once immaculately groomed woman was now changed, as if life no longer had meaning. Katharine touched her mother's hair and said, "Mother, we're going to get your hair done tomorrow. Is 'Betty's Beauty Temple' still operating in the village?"

They both laughed, but her mother's smile soon left. "I really don't need to bother anymore, Katie. No one sees me here."

"If I have anything to do with it they will."

Her mother walked out into the kitchen and put on the coffee. Little had changed, Katharine thought, except everything seemed to have a film of dust on it and needed refurbishing. She wandered into the large room at the back of the house which overlooked the sea and where they, as a family, had spent most of their time. The rumpled sofa still faced the sea and the window seat had masses of outdated magazines on it. The bookshelves were crammed with summer reading from past years. Instinctively she reached for her well-worn copy of Jane Austen's *Sense and Sensibility*—she would take it upstairs with her when she went to bed. It was an old friend.

Her mother returned with the coffee and some homemade cookies, baked especially for Katharine's visit. "I never seem to cook very much these days," she said wistfully.

"Well, you certainly should, Mother. You've lost a lot of weight. At least fifteen pounds?"

Sarah Hayes nodded. "Well," continued Katharine, "the next two days we are going to see to it that you take care of yourself. I want us to eat at the Clam Box and have all my old favorites. Remember when Dad and you used to dread taking us there? We always ate too much. . ."

Katharine stopped and their eyes met. Sarah Hayes' eyes filled with tears and Katharine whispered, "Oh, Mother . . ." Their arms were around one another and they cried softly together. Bruno jumped up, pawing them, distressed to see their sorrow.

Sarah Hayes broke away and dried her eyes. "Your coffee's getting cold, Katie."

Katharine picked up her cup and went over to sit on the window seat. It had been her special place. Curled up on it, she had watched the sea as the tides went in and out, leaving so many treasures to be found on the beach. Tomorrow, she would walk with Bruno and look for shells while she prayed to find the answer to her parents' situation.

Her mother's voice interrupted her thoughts. "Katie, we'll talk tomorrow, all right? I'm really exhausted and I know you must be. I want to hear all about the news program and how you're enjoying Washington. . ."

Katharine smiled. "I'm loving Washington, Mother."

"I'm glad." Sarah Hayes kissed her and walked to the foot of the stairs. With her hand on the railing, she said, "Your old room is waiting for you. It almost seems like old times, doesn't it, Katie?"

"Almost." Katharine was near to tears again. "Almost. Good night, Mother. I love you." She walked over and picked up the Jane Austen book. Running her fingers down its worn spine, she prayed silently that "old times" might return very soon.

Halfway up the stairs, she heard the telephone ring and wondered who could be calling so late.

It was Stephen. "Sorry to call at such an hour, but I figured you would only just be arriving. I wanted to be sure you got there safely."

Katharine felt a sense of joy go through her. "Oh, Stephen, thank you. The flight was fine and I managed the drive O.K."

"I miss you already."

"I miss you, too. I hope one day you can come up for a weekend. Tomorrow I'm going to walk on the beach with my dog..."

"I'll think of you, Katharine, and yes, I would love to come and share that beach with you one day soon." There was a pause. "I'm still remembering that last kiss, Katharine."

She closed her eyes for a moment. "Me too."

"Sleep well, dear Katharine. See you Sunday night. God bless."

Katharine whispered, "God bless *you*," and put the telephone down quietly. She turned to see her mother standing at the top of the stairs.

"Who was that, Katharine?"

"Stephen Douglass."

"*The* Stephen Douglass?"

"Yes, Mother. I interviewed him at the Capitol

the week before last and we've been seeing one
another. He took me to the airport...he just
wanted to see if I had arrived safely."

"How very considerate of him," her mother
said thoughtfully. "I've read he's a fine young
man."

"He is. I've grown very fond of him."

It was the first time she had voiced her feelings about Stephen to anyone. Now, as she began
to walk up the stairs, her face lit up with a ra-
diance her mother was quick to notice.

"I want you to meet him soon...."

Sense and Sensibility lay forgotten on the window seat.

Chapter Five

In spite of the late hour that she had finally fallen asleep, Katharine was on the beach by 7 A.M. Bruno had been delighted to see her ready for a walk and had excitedly rushed down the steps leading to the sand. There still was a chill despite it being summer. Washington's stifling heat seemed to overwhelm her sometimes, and Katharine thought how much she missed this invigorating, fresh air.

Sarah Hayes was still sleeping and had not heard Katharine leave, in spite of Bruno's delighted barking. He ran ahead panting, his old body still able to enjoy a run. Katharine threw a piece of driftwood and he ran over to it and shook it, growling his approval. She found a clam shell and brushed the sand off its curved sides, imagining how many miles it had traveled as it had been buffetted by the sea.

Her mother's face came to mind. Buffetted by the events of the past few weeks, lines had appeared and a sadness had invaded the once sparkling, beautiful gray-blue eyes. Katharine wondered what she could say to her mother that would bring back hope to this woman who had given her life and love to her family for so many happy years.

Katharine began to walk back to "Gull's Wings" and Bruno rushed on ahead, glad to be returning home. Sarah Hayes was waiting by the window, and when she saw Katharine wave she went back into the kitchen to finish cooking breakfast.

The brisk sea air had an almost heady effect on Katharine, and she burst into the old house renewed and determined that today would be a happy one for both of them. Her mother was cooking waffles and the aroma made Katharine realize just how hungry she was.

"Oh, Mother, it's such a glorious day. I don't want us to waste a minute!"

Sarah Hayes laughed and agreed that they should take advantage of every moment. Over breakfast, as Katharine started to talk about the impending divorce, her mother interjected, "I want to hear all about you first. Please, Katharine, I hear so little of your news." She filled Katharine's cup again with coffee and piled more waffles on her plate. Passing the maple syrup, she asked, "How is your work progressing?"

"I anchored for the first time last night," Katharine said triumphantly. "Owing to unfortunate circumstances, however—Sally Denton was taken ill and I was asked to stand in. I really enjoyed it, Mother. It just makes me all the more determined to get that position one day. If not in Washington, then some other city."

Even as she said this, her thoughts turned to Stephen. Always, before she had met him, she had felt free to work anywhere, but now she realized she would have second thoughts about leaving Washington purely for career reasons.

Sarah Hayes looked at her inquiringly. "Even if it meant not seeing your senator?"

"Mother, he's hardly *my* senator."

"I seem to detect a rather more than passing interest in him. On his part, it would seem he's very interested, considering he called to see if you were all right last night." Settling back in her chair, she said, "Tell me all about him."

Katharine's eyes lit up and she leaned forward, elbows on the table. "He's the most wonderful thing that has happened in my life! When I interviewed him at the Capitol I knew he had a depth to him—besides being so devastatingly attractive. We found out that we both were Christians. I can't tell you what a relief it was to be able to share my beliefs with someone who wasn't ready to pounce on me for being a 'Born

Againer'—one of those strange, narrow people who judge and condemn everyone else." Katharine sighed. "Mother, it's so sad, but that is what some people seem to think Christianity is all about."

"I know the media does have a way of bunching all us Christians into a tight little box and pointing the finger of condemnation. Perhaps it should make us all the more determined to live our lives as our Lord would have us do—loving, not condemning."

Katharine looked thoughtfully at her mother. "Is that what you are doing?"

Immediately, Sarah Hayes began to fold her napkin to avoid her daughter's questioning eyes. "I try not to condemn, you know that. I always have. But, Katharine, when your pride has been hurt so much and you feel that all your friends are talking about you, it's very hard to forgive and forget."

"How did you find out about Dad?"

"Kitty Merton told me."

"*That* suburban gossiper?"

"She said she saw him and this young woman dining at a restaurant in Greenwich. Kitty and her husband just happened to be eating there— they had never been there before. It was obvious to her that your dad was more than just friendly with the young woman."

"How was it obvious, Mother?"

"By the way he was looking at her."

"Mother, is this the only evidence you have about Dad?"

"No, he admitted he was seeing her. He said it had to do with his work, but I know there's more to it than that."

"Nowadays women do dine with men in connection with their work, so perhaps he was telling the truth."

Sarah Hayes exploded. "Then *why* didn't *he* tell me? Why did I have to find out from someone like Kitty Merton?" She jumped up and knocked her chair over. "I feel like such a fool. I can't go back to Greenwich. Everyone is gossiping about it."

Katharine went over to her mother and put her arms around her. "Dear, dear Mother, I think you have jumped to conclusions and it's not like the mother I used to know. You taught us to trust and love people. Something else must have happened to make you suddenly behave like this." She bent down and picked up the chair. Setting it in place, Katharine guided her mother to it and made her sit down.

"We're going to talk and have this out, Mother. Now, what would you say if I called Dad and asked him to come here so we could talk about all of this?"

"I would leave the house." Sarah Hayes' eyes were red-rimmed and defiant. "I don't want to talk to him. He's hurt me so deeply, I don't ever want to see him again."

"Is this the forgiving, loving person who I have always felt was a wonderful example of what a Christian should be?" Katharine took her hands. "Mother, I know how you must feel. I'm not condemning you. But you're only hurting yourself. I don't want you to be bitter. I want you to be free to love once more."

"Well, not *him*," her mother said angrily as she went into the kitchen with some of the breakfast dishes and put them noisily into the sink.

Katharine crossed to the bookshelf and found an old book of Tennyson's poems. One fall, Sarah Hayes had found this leather-bound book in an old book shop and had brought it home for Katharine. The family had often gathered around in the evening while Katharine sat cross-legged on the floor reading some of their favorite poetry. Ellen would be embroidering, urging her sister to recite a well-known poem.

Now, once again, she opened it to a poem they had often enjoyed.

Katharine walked into the kitchen and asked her mother to stop running the water for a moment and listen.

"Remember the night we all sat around and discussed this?"

> In Love, if Love be Love, if Love be ours,
> Faith and unfaith can ne'er be equal powers:
> Unfaith in aught is want of faith in all.

Katharine's mind turned to Stephen and she thought of his face, as he had watched her walk to the plane. Could it be that love was going to be theirs? Sarah Hayes dried her hands and stood looking out of the window, tears running down her face. Katharine immediately was brought back to the meaning of the poem for her mother.

> It is the little rift within the lute,
> That by and by will make the music mute,
> And ever widening slowly silence all.

> The little rift within the lover's lute
> Or little pitted speck in garnered fruit
> That rotting inward slowly moulders all.

> It is not worth the keeping: let it go:
> But shall it? answer, darling, answer, no.
> And trust me not at all or all in all.

Katharine put her arm around her mother and whispered, "Isn't your marriage 'worth the keeping'? You told us how important it was to have faith, to not let suspicions or doubts ruin relationships—whether they be with loved ones or friends, but most important of all to not let doubts destroy the joy of knowing our Lord's love." Katharine looked directly into her mother's eyes. "I realize, Mother, the love you had for Dad seems to have gone. But Jesus in you can love him and forgive him."

Sarah Hayes turned and hugged Katharine and put her head on her daughter's shoulder. Katharine hugged her in return and found herself thinking how the roles had reversed. It had been her mother, many years before, who had comforted her in this very kitchen once when she had thought her little world was coming to an end. It was so important to Katharine then, whatever it was that had happened—now all she could remember were her tears and the feeling of utter desolation.

"I love you, Mother, and I want you to promise me you are going to give your marriage a second chance." Sarah Hayes began to protest and Katharine went on, "If you can't promise at this moment, don't say anything, but let's really pray about it."

Together they quietly poured out their hearts, in the quiet of the room that had been such an important part of their lives.

"Help me to forget, Lord, and *forgive,*" Sarah began softly. The words came haltingly at first, then Katharine's mother began to speak from her heart and her daughter knew she was finally being freed of her bitterness.

"Thank you, dear Katie. I needed you so badly this weekend..."

"I'm glad I could be here, Mother." She kissed her cheek and pushing back some of the wisps of her mother's hair, she said, "Now, I'm going to call 'Betty's Beauty Temple' and see if I can get you an appointment!"

The tension was broken as they both laughed. The name of the little, unassuming shop had always been a joke in the family. On the telephone, Katharine was assured that one of Betty's "top beauty operators" would be free to work on Mrs. Hayes that morning.

They drove into the small town that was filled to capacity with summer residents and vacationers. Katharine left her mother at the "Temple," then wandered through the stores, trying to find a gift that might cheer up her mother. She looked across the busy street and saw "Vogue Fashions"—one of the classiest stores in town. In their window was a striking coral dress that would be perfect for her mother. She crossed the street and went in, asking whether the dress came in a size twelve. The one in the window was and after a few minutes it was being carefully wrapped in tissue paper, in the store's attractive violet-covered box and tied with a bright green satin bow. After paying for it, she walked out of the store, the box held under her arm.

Katharine glanced at her watch and saw that she still had over half an hour to wait for her mother, so she went into a charming little cafe for coffee. Sitting at a small table by the window, she watched the people walking by, but her thoughts were of Stephen. She wished he could be sitting across from her now—her day would be so different. There was an ache in her heart that not only came from the sorrow of her parents' separation, but the temporary separation from Stephen.

"I can't believe I could miss anyone quite so much," Katharine thought, stirring her coffee and toying with the Danish pastry she had ordered.

She turned to look around the cafe and noticed young couples engrossed in animated conversation, adding to her need to be with Stephen. She turned to a Greenwich newspaper she had bought and thumbing through it saw her photograph in the society column. They had picked up Julia Simpson's item about her and Stephen— now it said that local girl was making good in Washington. She read on:

> Since leaving Greenwich, Katharine Hayes has excelled as an investigative reporter for WNSC, Washington, D.C. It is obvious

that it is not only her career that is blos-
soming, but romance seems to be bloom-
ing for her, too. Senator Douglass comes
from a very prestigious family, with its
roots in the blue blood of old Virginia.

Katharine folded the paper and left the cafe.
She had never been able to get used to publicity
and now this really concerned her.

Someone was waving to her from across the
street and she realized it was Kitty Merton, who
had spread the gossip about her father. Katharine turned to ignore her, but Kitty's insistent
voice made her turn back. Kitty rushed across
the street, halting traffic with a forbidding hand,
shouting, "Katharine, darling, I'm so *thrilled* for
you!"

She kissed Katharine on the cheek and to Katharine it felt like a vulture pecking at its prey.

"Do tell me all about Stephen Douglass. I hear
he is really much more handsome than even his
photographs. You certainly haven't let any grass
grow under your feet since you got to Washington, dear Katharine."

"We are only friends, Kitty, and I do mean
friends," Katharine tried to convince her, but
Kitty would have none of it. She smiled at Katharine ingratiatingly and patted her cheek. "I'm
really happy for you, really..."

"As happy as you were to spread stories about

my father?" Katharine could not resist facing her with her damaging gossip.

Kitty's expression changed and with a glint in her eyes, she said emphatically, "Too bad your mother couldn't keep hold of your father. I only wish I could have got to him first." She turned and walked up the street triumphantly, not concerned about having hurt someone—delighted in her seemingly victorious encounter.

Katharine stood watching her leave, angry and near to tears. She walked back into the cafe and without hesitating found a quarter in her handbag, then dialed the family home in Greenwich, praying that her father would be there. After a few rings, she was about to hang up when she heard his voice.

"Hello?"

Katharine was overjoyed. "Dad, it's Katie."

"How wonderful to hear your voice. I've just been reading about you in the newspaper. Where are you?"

"In Mystic, waiting for Mother to come out of the hairdresser's. I'm up for the weekend. Dad, do you think you could drive over this evening?"

"Katie, I don't think I would be welcome."

"*Please.* I think you and Mother should talk. Perhaps with me there, it wouldn't be quite so difficult. I can always take Bruno for a walk if things seem to be going well."

Her father paused for some time. "She told me she never wanted to see me again. I have to respect her wishes."

"I believe things are going to be different." Katharine told him about her conversation with her mother earlier that morning. "I don't promise any overnight reconciliation, but I do think the door is slightly open now."

"Katie, there never was anything serious with this girl. I hope you believe that."

"I want to, Dad. I have always loved and respected you, you know that. You and Mother belong together. I came up because I couldn't bear to think of you two being apart. And, besides, the gate at "Gull's Wings" needs fixing!"

"Oh, well in that case, I had better come over, hadn't I?" His voice expressed the humor she had always associated with him, even in times of crisis. "I'll come, Katie. I'll come," he said quietly. "Just don't expect any miracles."

"That's too bad, Dad, because... I do."

Katharine put the receiver down and noticed that her hand was shaking. She bit her lip and walked out of the cafe, in the direction of the hairdresser's. Her mother was walking out of the door and she looked so much more like her old self. Her lustrous brown hair, with the golden lights in it, shone once more and was styled softly around her still beautiful face.

"You look lovely, Mother, really lovely," Katharine said admiringly. They walked back to the car arm in arm, Katharine telling her that the gift she bought was for that evening and that her mother could not look at it until they got back home.

Bruno ran out to meet them as they walked up the steps of the old house. Katharine led her mother over to the window seat and handing her the box, she said, "Now you may open it, but you have to promise me you will wear whatever is in there."

"I promise, I promise," her mother said excitedly.

When she saw the lovely coral dress, she exclaimed, "Katie, you shouldn't have. . ." Then looking at her, she said, "But, I'm so glad you did!" Sarah Hayes rushed over to the hall mirror and put the dress up to her. "I love it, I really do. I'm going to save it for a very special occasion."

Katharine said determinedly, "No, I want you to wear it tonight."

"But why?"

"Well, maybe we'll go out and eat. I brought a dress with me and it seems a shame not to have us both go out somewhere."

Her mother finally agreed and decided that after lunch she would do her nails and take a nap, so she would look her very best that evening.

•　•　•

Katharine was sitting watching the sea, later that afternoon. She wondered if she had done the right thing, having called her father. Would it prove to be embarrassing for each of them? She had felt some kind of action was necessary before returning to Washington, so perhaps it was better to do the wrong thing than nothing at all.

The telephone rang and immediately Katharine thought it was her father calling to tell her he had changed his mind. But it was Stephen.

"I can't believe it's you," Katharine said breathlessly.

"Well, it is. I am finding this to be an exceptionally long day without you, so the next best thing is to hear your voice. Anyway, I do have an invitation to extend to you—from my mother."

"Oh, really?" Katharine sat down rather suddenly. Mrs. Douglass was one person she dreaded meeting, but she managed to say, "How nice."

"She would like you to come for lunch next Sunday and spend the rest of the day. Will you be free?"

"As far as I know, Stephen. Please thank her for me."

"I will. How are things going, Katharine? Are you alone?"

"Yes," she said lowering her voice. "Things are going well, I think. I have asked Dad to come over this evening. Mother doesn't know about it yet so, please, do pray."

"I will, Katharine. I know what this means to you."

Katharine heard her mother's footsteps at the top of the stairs and quickly altered her tone of voice. "The air here is so wonderful. I ran on the beach with Bruno this morning..."

Stephen sensed that she could not talk freely and said, "I frankly can't wait to see you tomorrow evening. Mother has a charity committee meeting going on right now, so I'm going for a ride." He whispered, "Miss you and know I'll be praying with you. God bless, dear Katharine."

"God bless and thank you..."

She hung up the telephone and called out to her mother, "It was Stephen again!"

Sarah Hayes called back, "How delightful, Katie."

•   •   •

That evening as Katharine and her mother were finishing dressing, they heard a hammering sound coming from the driveway. Looking out of her bedroom window, Katharine saw that her father was mending the gate and she waved to him. He waved back, just as her mother came into Katharine's room.

"Who are you waving to?"

Katharine's mother peered out of the window and saw her husband in the distance. Turning to look at Katharine, she said, "You terror, Katie Hayes. You have engineered this whole thing." Looking down at the coral dress, she touched the lace around the cuffs. "I should be angry with you..."

Their eyes met and Katharine put her arms out to her mother.

"Forgive me?"

They walked toward one another and Sarah Hayes put her arms around her daughter. "You always were the one who wouldn't take 'no' for an answer."

Katharine whispered, "And I'm not about to change now!"

Chapter Six

Katharine walked straight into Stephen's arms as he waited for her at the barrier. Her plane had been delayed for an hour in New York, due to thunderstorms, but she had managed to telephone him before he left Virginia for the airport. The warmth of his arms around her now gave her a feeling of assurance that no matter what happened in her life, Stephen would be there to protect and love her. She felt the excitement of his face against hers as he whispered, "Welcome home, Katharine."

They walked arm in arm out of the airport, conscious of people looking at them, but overjoyed to be together again.

"It seemed like the longest weekend I have ever spent. Katharine Hayes, you are rapidly changing my whole life!"

Katharine exclaimed, "I felt as if part of me were still here in Washington with you."

Stephen kissed her again, as he opened the

door of his station wagon. "We have a lot of talking to do. I want to hear about *everything* that happened in Connecticut. Then I have some very good news for you."

"Oh, tell me the good news first," Katharine insisted, as she fastened her seat belt.

Stephen looked at her and said, "You know you are the most lovely woman I ever met. How did a girl from Connecticut get to be so beautiful? We Southerners are supposed to have all the 'belles.' "

"Virginia isn't the *Deep* South, Senator."

Stephen grinned and pulled out into the evening airport traffic, concentrating on his driving.

"You still haven't told me the good news. . . ." Katharine insisted.

"Well, I talked on the phone with my brother Rick and he is all for giving a free concert for the inner-city kids."

"Oh, Stephen, that's wonderful! Now all we have to do is find the right place. Do you think we could get the parking lot and supermarket cleared that I was telling you about? The supermarket could be turned into a clubhouse for them and I know we could get volunteers to help run it!"

Katharine's enthusiasm spilled over as she pictured the happiness of the children and Stephen turned to look at her animated face.

"I'm sure we can arrange something, Miss Organizer. I'll make some calls tomorrow and let you know what I can come up with."

"Oh, thank you! When will Rick be here?"

"In about two weeks. After his big concert at Constitution Hall, he's going to stay for a while. Sort of a vacation for him. Now, please, tell me what happened between your parents."

Katharine settled back in her seat and relayed all that had transpired between her and her mother and then of the arranged meeting with her father.

"Mother was really shaken when she looked out of the window and saw Dad. I thought at first she was going to refuse to see him, but when she went downstairs and opened the front door and he was standing out there on the porch, something seemed to happen between them. They still aren't back together, but they have promised that they will go to our church for counseling. It's a first step but, Stephen, I am so thankful. I have never seen two people more miserable than my parents without each other."

Stephen squeezed Katharine's hand. "We'll keep praying. Your love for them must have meant so much. This really all came about because of gossip, didn't it?" Katharine nodded. He remarked thoughtfully, "It's not only in this town that lives are destroyed by it."

Katharine told him about the poem by Tennyson that she had read to her mother. "It always brings home to me the importance of trusting one another."

Stephen, his eyes on the road ahead, said quietly, "Recite some of it for me..."

She hesitated for a moment, then began:

> In Love, if Love be Love, if Love be ours,
> Faith and unfaith can ne'er be equal powers...

"If love be ours," Stephen said thoughtfully. "Do you think there are any 'ifs' in our relationship, Katharine?"

Katharine did not answer him straight away—being in love seemed so new, so fragile to her. "At this moment—no," she said huskily.

Stephen drove into a turnoff overlooking the Potomac and parked the car. They sat looking at the tranquilly beautiful scene, his hand in hers. After a few seconds, Stephen said, "I've never felt this way about anyone else, Katharine. I don't believe there are any 'ifs.' Somehow I feel very sure you're the person I have been consciously waiting for all this time."

Katharine put her head on his shoulder saying, almost inaudibly, "I think we have just found something else to pray about. If we *are* meant for each other, then God is going to make it very clear to us, isn't He?" She thought for a few seconds, and then said, "I seem to have such tremendous faith in you. In a way that I have never had in any other man . . ."

They turned to look at each other and Katharine saw that Stephen's eyes were misted over. He touched her hair and said, "I know we have only known each other such a short time, yet I feel it has been a lifetime. How can I thank the Lord enough for bringing you to me, Katharine?"

She kissed him gently on the cheek. "I have so much to thank Him for . . ." They sat silently, locked in each other's arms. Katharine felt tears in her eyes as she thanked the Lord for this remarkably sensitive and loving man, who had such strong ideals and a love for all that she believed in.

Stephen brushed the tears from her eyes. "We have so much to look forward to . . . Katie." The tender nickname her parents called her made even more tears come to her eyes.

"Forgive me. No one calls me that name now except my family."

"Do you mind if I call you that?"

"Of course I don't. I would love you to . . . I'm not going to call you Steve, however. Stephen has always been a name I have loved. It stands for a man of courage, a man who wasn't afraid to face his enemies for what he believed."

Stephen looked down at her. "He was my ideal, too, when I was growing up. His belief in our Lord always inspired me." Stephen brought her close to him again. "I love you, dear Katie."

"And I love you," she whispered, "and always will." They kissed and Katharine felt the warmth of his love surge through her. She knew in her heart that this was the man with whom she wanted to share the rest of her life. But, with a touch of reality, she realized all that it would imply. A man of his position and social standing. And his mother, no doubt, had a very set idea of the woman she wanted her son to marry.

Thoughts were swirling around in Katharine's head and she felt almost dizzy from them. Next Sunday she would be meeting Mrs. Douglass, whose stern reputation had preceded her. Katharine wondered if she would make a good impression.

"What were you thinking about?" Stephen asked gently.

"Senator, I'm going to take the 'Fifth' on that one, if you don't mind!" Katharine looked away, a smile breaking on her lips. "Let me say I'm not thinking very rationally at the moment. My head is spinning and my heart is pounding so loudly, I can't be held responsible for my thoughts."

"Well, I can and I think right now we should

get out of this car and walk for a while." He kissed her and held her close, then said breathlessly, "For a man who always has to control his feelings and represent his constituents in a calm, rational way, all I can say is—I'm glad I don't have to be speaking in the Senate at this hour!"

They got out of the car and began to walk along the river, Stephen's arm tightly around her shoulders. Katharine felt that this was the most perfect night of her life. The Potomac River glided smoothly by them. Yachts and small boats were returning from weekend "get-away" excursions. Voices from them drifted across the water to the couple as they leaned over the wall, stopping to watch the beautiful sight.

He looked over at Katharine, the fading sunlight reflecting in her golden hair. "You're beautiful, Katie." His strong, virile arms were around her once more and they clung to each other, both deeply conscious that this was a new beginning, an important moment they would always remember.

Katharine tilted her head back to look once more into his electrifyingly compelling eyes, that seemed to store all the joy and sorrow of his convictions. "What are your dreams, Stephen?" she asked, seeing in him a man who seemed to ache many times for all the pain and need that he saw in the world.

He thought for a moment, then leaning against the wall he looked back at the panorama of Washington. To the left was the Lincoln Memorial, a monument to a man who had envisioned dreams and had seen many fulfilled, but at great cost to his private life. In the distance the Washington Monument soared magnificently into the sky.

"Katie, I look at this city with all its reminders of our history, reminders of the cost of freedom, and I pray that I might in some way contribute to making this country what our Founding Fathers envisioned. We have come a long way, but I see so many inequities that need righting."

His young face took on an expression that reminded Katharine of those she had seen in portraits at the National Gallery—of men who had dedicated their whole lives to the service of their country. There was a resoluteness about Stephen that almost alarmed her. Could she live up to all that would be required of a woman who would share this exceptional man's life?

Katharine began to question her own ambitions. Were they in the right perspective? Had she put her commitment to God first, or was hers a purely selfish ambition?

"Why so pensive, Katie?"

"I suppose when I look at this overwhelmingly moving scene, I realize my life is very shallow."

Stephen took her into his arms. "Shallow? Hardly. I see a young woman who is contributing so much in a very positive way. I'm very glad you are where you are. You can influence the world with your caring. Don't downgrade yourself, Katie. I do believe our Lord has charted a very special course for you."

They began to walk again. Hand in hand, they were oblivious to others who walked by, content to be absorbed in each other for these peaceful moments. Tomorrow they would face the world again, but this evening they had each other and Katharine thought, "It is more than I ever dreamed of. . . ."

●　　●　　●

Upon parting the previous evening, they had planned to meet for lunch the next day at the Senate. Now Katharine dressed painstakingly, wanting to look her best for Stephen.

Connie had called to tell her that she would be anchoring for the next two weeks. The suspected appendicitis had proved to be a false alarm, but Sally Denton was taking time off to recuperate. Now Katharine looked forward to this time of anchoring. It would be a good opportunity, as far as her career was concerned.

The day was still one of stifling heat, so she chose a filmy, light cotton floral dress, reminiscent of the Edwardian era. Its beige background matched her high-heeled pumps, and as she looked into her full-length mirror she sensed that Stephen would admire her outfit.

"Perhaps this is the dress I should save for Sunday," she thought. It had the right, decorous look in which to meet his mother. She hesitated, looking through her other dresses. Then quickly she decided that she would wear this one today and buy another dress in which to impress Mrs. Douglass. Katharine looked over at the brass carriage clock on the mantlepiece and saw it was time to leave for her luncheon appointment.

Traffic was almost at a standstill and this was the part of Washington that she could never get used to. In Greenwich she could always count on being on time; but here, well, she decided to sit back and think calmly about eventually being with Stephen. It was almost noon when she reached the Senate Office Building. After pushing her way through the glass doors that led to Stephen's office, she encountered his secretary Maggie, regally sitting at her desk— looking like a proud lioness, jealously guarding her domain.

"Good morning, I have an appointment with the Senator."

Maggie looked disdainfully through the appointment book.

"I have no record of such an appointment, Ms...."

Katharine knew very well that Maggie was aware of who she was, but she smiled anyway. "Hayes."

"But of course...*Ms.* Hayes."

Katharine had never really cared about being called "Ms." Now she liked it even less when Maggie made it sound like some beleaguered mosquito about to sting its unsuspecting quarry. Katharine noted that Maggie was immaculately groomed in a very chic, expensive suit—her hair swept back, with not a wisp out of place.

"One moment, I'll see if he can speak with you." Maggie buzzed Stephen's office and told him, "A Ms. Hayes is here to see you. Are you expecting her?"

The door from Stephen's office opened almost immediately. He came racing over to Katharine and kissed her on the cheek, much to the chagrin of Maggie, whose face had turned scarlet. Not with embarrassment, but anger.

"Maggie, I'll be in the Senate dining room if anything comes up that needs my immediate attention. But, please, only if it's a matter of life and death. I would like to enjoy an uninterrupted lunch with Miss Hayes."

Katharine walked out of the office with him, sensing Maggie's disapproving eyes upon them.

She called out, "I have to call your mother about some rather pressing matters. Do you have any message for her, Senator?"

Stephen called back over his shoulder, "No, just tell her I'll be calling later today, Maggie. Thanks..." and he walked quickly down the hallway, whispering to Katharine how fantastic she looked.

The dining room was crowded when they arrived. Many familiar faces turned to look at them as they were escorted to their table.

"I highly recommend the navy bean soup—a traditional staple here since the 1800s. On the other hand, the weather seems to suggest a lighter fare, don't you think?" Stephen was in a happy, jovial mood, as he held her hand and kept gazing at her. "Remarkably beautiful, that's what you are, darling Katie."

Katharine smiled and thanked him and then waved to another senator, who had been trying to attract her attention. Stephen swung around to see to whom she was waving and said incredulously, "I didn't know you knew Dennis Fraser—he's one of the senators in our prayer group that meets each week."

Katharine looked surprised. "I interviewed him several weeks ago. He seemed to be a very understanding, compassionate man."

"He is. I could go to Dennis with any problem

and I know he would listen and care." Stephen suddenly exclaimed, "What a great idea! Excuse me a moment," and before Katharine knew what was happening he had raced over to Dennis Fraser's table and was deep in conversation with him. Once or twice they looked back at Katharine, who had no idea what they were discussing. She saw Stephen slap Senator Fraser on the back, then return to their table and sit down, looking rather triumphant.

Katharine looked at him questioningly. "And what was all that about?" she said, intrigued by what had transpired.

"Dennis has agreed to help us with Rick's concert for the children. In fact, he has a few ideas of how to get that supermarket and parking lot cleared and is getting to it immediately after lunch. Not with a broom, mind you, but he's going to make some phone calls."

Katharine was delighted. "That's really wonderful!" She looked across at Senator Fraser and mouthed a silent "Thank you." He smiled back, indicating he would come over to them when he had finished his meal.

"That's given me more ideas. Our prayer group wants to get involved in some kind of project. I can just see us all really getting this thing off the ground."

As they ate lunch, Stephen was elated, full of

ideas and wishing they could start immediately.

Katharine put her hand on his arm, "Steady, Senator, your blood pressure is soaring and you have a busy afternoon ahead of you."

Stephen had been asked to head a subcommittee on international human rights and was eager to see that questions of possible violations were not just swept aside. "I have seen it happen too many times, Katharine." His face changed expression. With determination, he said, "We cannot remain silent."

Katharine had done a special investigative report on the subject—in fact, it had been recently rerun and had created great interest in Washington. "I would like to listen in on this afternoon's proceedings, but I have to get back to the studio."

"I'll tell you how it went when I pick you up at the studio tonight," Stephen assured her. "Unless, of course, we go into secret session."

Senator Fraser approached the table, smiling at Katharine and shaking her hand. "What a great idea of yours, Miss Hayes. I have really been looking for something to do like this. We need to reach out and get involved with the problems in this immediate area. We shall have to meet and discuss all the possibilities. Stephen says you are interested in starting some kind of center for these children."

Katharine said eagerly, "Yes, there is so much potential for good. It would be a real need that would be met. I feel we cannot just say 'Jesus loves you' and walk on by, ignoring the fact that these children are hurting."

"Exactly," Stephen said emphatically. "You cannot expect them to listen if they feel no one is interested in their well-being."

Senator Fraser joined them for coffee and they spent the last fifteen minutes of the lunch hour discussing tactics and making concrete plans. Katharine glanced at her watch and said she would have to be leaving.

"Me, too," Stephen said realizing the time. "I'll walk you back to the garage—I have a few minutes before I need to get to the committee room."

They said good-bye to Senator Fraser, promising they would all get together soon and get down to something tangible.

As they walked out of the dining room they ran into a camera crew from Katharine's television station. They smiled and a cameraman whispered, "I thought we had already interviewed the Senator!"

Katharine looked him straight in the eye and said with a grin, "We did. See you tonight."

Stephen overheard the conversation and smiled at the camera crew. "Good to see you all again." Under his breath he said, "You'll never know how thankful I am your Miss Hayes interviewed me." He looked over at Katharine and their eyes locked warmly, betraying their feelings to the crew.

Stephen and Katharine walked under the great rotunda with the glorious Brumidi frescoe—a fitting tribute to George Washington. Visitors were lined up to start a tour of the Capitol and Katharine almost wished she could join them. She always found the magnificent building inspiring. Some of the visitors recognized Stephen and Katharine. Heads began to turn and tongues wagged, as they became excited to see these celebrities.

Stephen smiled and waved at several of them as he whisked her past them and eventually to the long corridor, which led to the underground garage. It was deserted and Stephen took Katharine in his arms and kissed her.

"I love this old Capitol building, but it sure doesn't have much privacy."

"Definitely not a place for 'courting.' " Katharine put her arms around his neck. "I love you, Stephen. Thank you for lunch. I . . ."

He stopped her with another kiss and they stood locked in each other's arms, thankful for a few private moments alone.

It was Katharine who finally broke away.

"Regretfully, I do have to go." They walked on and found her car. Once inside, she rolled down the window and Stephen leaned in and kissed her au revoir.

"See you tonight and why don't we drive by that parking lot and supermarket, before we go to eat?"

"A great idea! Yes, I'll take you by and show you my dream..." Katharine smiled up at him and blew him a kiss.

Stephen whispered, "I love you, Katie. Take care. God bless."

Reluctantly, Katharine started the engine and drove out of the garage. In her rearview mirror, she could see Stephen standing there, watching her leave and she waved to him.

"I can't believe I have found this man, Lord. It's almost too wonderful...."

Chapter Seven

Although the news program went well that night, Katharine found herself feeling more tense than when she had anchored Friday night. The uneasy relationship between Alan and herself seemed to be heightening. He had given her very terse instructions before going on the air and the rest of the news team had noticed it—commenting that "Our news director must have had a bad weekend."

Katharine knew that what was building up in Alan was strictly because of how he felt about her. She wondered if she should speak to him privately, but as soon as the news program finished he had left the studio.

"In 'high dudgeon,' " Connie had commented. "I once read that phrase in an English Victorian novel and didn't know what it really meant. I'm still not sure, but I think it means 'angry.' In any event, it seems to fit his mood, Miss Hayes. Don't worry—you were great."

"Thank you, Connie. I really appreciate that."

The young girl's personality always managed to brighten the darkest of days in the newsroom, and as Katharine walked back to her dressing room she thanked the Lord once more for the presence of Connie.

Stephen would be waiting for Katharine outside—they had decided not to inflame Alan any more than was necessary. Now as she approached the exit doors her heart began to beat faster. He would help her put this whole thing in the right perspective. As soon as she saw him leaning against his station wagon a feeling of relief, mixed with excitement, overtook her. She ran into his arms and felt his lips on hers, making the pressures of the world disappear for a few idyllic seconds.

"Hi, sweet Kate—I thought the hours would never pass by until we were together again."

Katharine did not say anything, just looked into his eyes—hers brimming with tears.

"Hey, what's wrong?"

Katharine could not speak, but got into the station wagon and Stephen closed the door. As he got in on the driver's side, she whispered, "Let's drive away from here and then I'll tell you."

Stephen drove quietly for a few blocks, past the floodlit, majestic, white marble Supreme Court Building, reminiscent of a Greek temple.

The sparkling fountain outside completed the magnificent scene. In sharp contrast, within a few blocks, the overgrown, garbage-strewn, derelict parking lot and supermarket came into view.

Stephen parked the car opposite and sat looking at the depressing scene. Though it was nearly midnight, some teenagers were playing kickball amid the rubbish. Others sat on the steps of the old supermarket, listlessly looking into space.

"This is your dream?" Stephen asked Katharine somberly.

The sight of the teenagers caused Katharine to forget her immediate problems. "Yes," she said emphatically. "Can't you picture it cleared and painted? It would make a wonderful recreation center for them."

Stephen looked at her earnest face. There were both tears and determination in her eyes. "I share your dream, Katie." He took her hand as he said, "Let's pray about it . . . and *you*."

The warmth of his hand in hers and his prayer restored Katharine's confidence. "Now, please tell me what's wrong, Katie."

"I'm fine," she assured him. "Rather annoyed with myself for letting things get me down." She told him of Alan's behavior. "I know that when you're in this business you are supposed to have a hide like a rhinoceros. I just wish I could grow one overnight." She thought for a minute. "Stephen, do you really think I'm the right personality for television?"

"Of course. Don't let criticism get you down. You are so good—so seemingly assured. Katie, anyone who is willing to stick his or her neck up above the crowd has to be prepared for criticism and strange reactions from people." He laughed rather thoughtfully. "I could write a book about *my* detractors."

Stephen looked across the road at the dejected teenagers. "Imagine how they must feel most of the time and we are fortunate enough to be in a position to perhaps help them. Don't give up, beautiful lady. When the Lord gives you a burden, He always supplies the strength to carry it through."

"Thank you, dear Stephen. You always make me feel better." She flung her arms around him, as he went to start the car. He leaned forward and kissed her and once again she was thankful for the assurance of his love and beliefs.

"I'm going to take you somewhere, where we can relax and eat something. I want you to forget the cares of your fellow human beings for a while, otherwise you won't be any use to anyone."

They went to a small bistro in Georgetown and

Katharine found herself laughing once more. "I do take myself too seriously, don't I?"

"We all do at times," Stephen said while passing her the butter. "Remember, you are coming with me to Virginia on Sunday?"

"I remember only too well," Katharine replied jokingly. "I've already rehearsed my opening conversation with your mother a hundred times."

Stephen took her hand reassuringly. "It's not as if you were going to your execution, you know," he said laughingly. Then he asked, "I was wondering if we could take your niece and nephew to the zoo on Saturday?"

"Oh, yes, that would be wonderful. I'll call Ellen tomorrow morning and see if they can go. You'll really love them. When I'm with those two I forget everything else. Jamie will talk your ear off and Beth will adore you."

"I just hope her aunt does," Stephen said in a low voice.

Katharine put her hand in his. "You don't have to hope, Stephen . . . she already does."

The candlelight cast a radiant glow across her face, making her look even more beautiful. The brilliant blue eyes sparkled. Being with Stephen had made her forget her encounter at the studio already.

When they had finished their meal, they

walked for a while along the quaint, historic, tree-lined streets of Georgetown which provided a quiet, romantic background. Each house had a particular personality of its own—the painted shutters, the front doors with brass knockers, the window boxes, and some houses with small front yards adorned with colorful flowers. They were all visible reminders of the past.

Katharine looked in one of the windows as they walked by. A lamp cast a dim light and she could just make out the small, inviting living room. Two people were silhouetted as they conversed together.

"Would you like to come back to my place for some more coffee?" Katharine asked Stephen.

"It's late, but maybe just for half an hour. Why don't we go and get Blarney, so he can enjoy it, too?"

Katharine eagerly concurred and as Stephen took her hand they ran down the street toward his home. Blarney was delighted to see his master and made a great fuss over Katharine, too. They found it hard to restrain him at first, then with his leash on, he led them at a quick pace along the cobblestone streets to Katharine's house. Stephen would get his car from the bistro parking lot later.

The geraniums, in the stone urn on the top step

outside her front door, were looking wilted—
the leaves and petals drooping from the heat.

"Oh, dear, I forgot to water them this morning," Katharine said regretfully.

"Where's the watering can? I'll attend to it,"
Stephen volunteered.

"It's right by the back door," she called over
her shoulder, while preparing the coffee.

The night was still and the heat of the day had
subsided, making it perfect for sitting in the
garden. Next door, a stereo was playing some
hauntingly romantic music.

"I ordered that especially," Katharine remarked with a laugh.

"It's perfect," Stephen said as he came and sat
down beside her. "I'm glad your neighbors are
night owls, too." He kissed her and coffee was
completely forgotten until, quite abruptly, Blarney put his two front paws on Katharine's lap
and demanded her attention.

"I do believe he's jealous of me," Stephen said.
"Shame on you for interrupting . . ." He ordered
Blarney down and stroking him, he said, "It's
worse than having a chaperone around, old
fella!"

Stephen put his arm around Katharine once
more and they enjoyed a few more minutes in
the marvel of their love.

●　　●　　●

The week passed by without too much drama at the studio. Alan had retreated somewhat. Heads of the network were in town and everyone was on his best behavior. Strange faces were seen in the corridor and on the sound stage. Katharine had been introduced to several of them who were very appreciative of her work.

Plans for the children's center were progressing well and several telephone calls from Stephen and Senator Fraser had succeeded in their being able, along with several other benefactors, to lease the property on a monthly basis.

In addition, plans were now in operation to remove the garbage and a schedule had been set up for volunteers to start painting the old supermarket. Sports equipment was being donated and Katharine was amazed by the generosity of so many people.

She had received a telephone call from her mother, who told her she and Katharine's father had begun their counseling sessions.

"There is still so much for me to get over, Katie, I don't know if I can ever have faith in your father again." But the door was still open and Katharine prayed, very positively, that they would one day be reunited.

"Nothing is impossible for you, Lord. Give them Your love for each other...."

Saturay morning dawned and Katharine had completed arrangements to take Jamie and Beth to the zoo with Stephen. He would be meeting her at the old supermarket, then, after painting for a few hours, they would drive out to Bethesda and pick up the children.

Katharine felt elated as she dressed in jeans and a colorful plaid shirt. She would continue to feel this way since she would be with Stephen. The thought of him meeting some of her family made her feel especially happy.

Before driving over to the supermarket, she stopped off at the Library of Congress, where she needed to study for a report that would shortly be coming up for Columbus Day. The impressive building always had an awesome effect on her. High up in the dome were the words from Micah 6:8, that had so touched her the first time she visited the library:

> . . . What doth the Lord require of thee,
> but to do justly, and to love mercy, and
> to walk humbly with thy God?

Each time she looked up at those words they seemed to speak to her in a penetrating way. *Was* she walking humbly with God? So much of her time was, of necessity, spent thinking about her career, her ambitions for the future. The very nature of her work forced her to have

confidence in her abilities. Katharine knew she
had not devoted enough time to her relationship
with the Lord—always other events seemed to
crowd out the moments she could spend quietly
meditating on His love.

A library assistant asking if she could help
Katharine brought her thoughts back to the
reason she had come to the library. She re-
quested several books and while she waited for
them, she glanced around the vast building. The
hushed air, with just an occasional whisper coming from an assistant helping one of the public,
gave the building an even more awesome atmosphere.

Finally, the librarian returned and whispered
to Katharine that some of her requests were out
on loan at the moment, but she was handed the
rest. Katharine thanked her quietly and walked
to a desk, where she gently pulled in her chair
so as not to make a noise. Several people around
her looked up, then returned to their studies—
the only sounds coming from a pencil or pen as
they made notes, a cough here and there.

Katharine became so engrossed in her search
for interesting facts pertaining to Columbus, that
she was hardly aware that someone had come
and sat down beside her. A quick glance out of
the corner of her eye revealed a rather grubby-
looking person, dressed in shabby jeans, a shirt

that had seen better days and a well-worn base-ball cap crammed down on its owner's head. Dark glasses completed the outfit and Katharine wondered what this man could possibly be studying. He reached into one of his pockets, brought out an apple, and took a bite—which sounded like cannon fire roaring through the library.

"Wanna bite, lady?" he asked and shoved the offending apple up to her face.

"No, thank you," Katharine whispered, not looking at him and trying not to make a scene. Now she felt eyes upon her as those seated nearby watched with growing annoyance.

"It's a great apple," the man said in a gruff voice.

"I said, no, thank you."

Katharine looked down at her books and felt her face begin to redden. She wished this man would go away. He put down the apple in front of her and it was then that she recognized the ring on his right hand. It was Stephen's college ring!

Katharine tried to conceal her laughter and she bit her lip while tears began to form. A giggle emerged and she closed the books, leaving them on the desk, grabbed her notes, and raced out of the library with Stephen in full chase. Out-side, Katharine could not stop laughing.

"Stephen, you are the worst, the absolute worst. I thought I was going to explode in there." Tears were still rolling down her face and they held hands and laughed together.

"Thought you might need some diversion. After all, it *is* Saturday—you can't work all the time."

"I never would have recognized you, but for your ring," Katharine said incredulously. "Do you often use this disguise?"

"Many times. Especially when I go shopping. Do you know, I actually saw the Secretary of Defense pushing his cart in our local Safeway? Walked right past him and he didn't recognize me. I noticed he had bought several frozen chicken pies and wondered what effect they would have on his judgment!"

Katharine hit him playfully with her handbag and he grabbed her on the steps of the library and kissed her, as people climbed the steps and looked disdainfully at them.

"I didn't think I would dress up anyway as we are going to paint at the center and then go to the zoo."

Katharine walked with him to the station wagon, looking at him again out of the corner of her eye. "Do you have any other clothes to change into?" she said hopefully.

"Don't worry, I won't let you down in front

of your family, Katie. I brought another pair of shoes with me."

She looked down and saw the absolutely oldest sneakers she had ever seen. "I should hope so," and with that they started to laugh again.

Driving over to the youth-center-to-be, she thought again of how much she loved to be with him. He was often serious, deeply committed to his work, but he had these wonderfully surprising lighter moments that brought her such a feeling of joy.

They spent about two hours at the center, splashing on paint and talking with the volunteers that had shown up. Many of the volunteers were familiar faces around Washington and Katharine thought of the possibility of doing a story some time, showing the caring side of these famous people. Even some of the local teenagers were lending a hand, which really gladdened Katharine.

She and Stephen grabbed a quick hamburger at a nearby stand and decided they would have to change clothes when they arrived at Ellen's home in Bethesda.

"She will probably wonder who is arriving. Ellen is always, I mean *always*, immaculate. You could surprise her scrubbing the kitchen floor and she still would look immaculate!"

As the station wagon drove up the driveway,

Jamie and Beth, who had been waiting in the front yard, came bounding up to Katharine and Stephen. Katharine hugged them both.

"I have been looking forward all week to our trip to the zoo."

"So have we!" they chorused in unison. "We thought you would never get here."

Katharine introduced the children to Stephen, who had at least changed his shoes and taken off his battered hat. Paint was visible on most parts of his old clothing.

"It's great to meet you—your Aunt Katharine has been telling me all kinds of terrific things about you."

Beth jumped up and down and Jamie took Stephen's hand and shook it over and over again.

Ellen came out and was slightly surprised to see how her sister and her companion were dressed. "Don't worry, Ellen, we do have other clothes in which to be seen with your children," Katharine assured her.

Her sister was immaculately dressed, as predicted. Ellen's dark brown hair shone lustrously in the sunlight, contrasting harmoniously with the well-cut gold jump suit she was wearing. Both sisters were very attractive and Stephen was quick to notice this.

"The Hayes Family certainly has beautiful daughters."

Ellen thanked him and invited him into her home, which was almost identical to the family home in Connecticut, only much smaller.

Laughingly, Katharine filled Ellen in about the library and the practical joke Stephen had pulled there. The children were enjoying listening to the story, too, when they were interrupted by their father arriving home from the Pentagon. Dressed in his officer's uniform, Colonel Jim Bartlett contrasted vividly with Stephen's shabby attire.

Katharine smiled across at him and introduced Stephen as someone she had picked up that morning in the Library of Congress. Jim, who was known for his dry sense of humor, remarked that surely she could have done better on skid row, while shaking Stephen's hand warmly in welcome.

The children were bursting to be on their way to the zoo, so Katharine and Stephen went their respective ways and quickly changed. The transformation was amazing. Katharine had brought a beautifully tailored pair of white pants and a blue cotton blouse that complimented her eyes. Stephen changed into some respectable jeans and a white cotton polo shirt. As he talked with Ellen and Jim, Katharine admired his fabulous physique. Tennis most mornings before he went to the Hill kept Stephen in excellent physical shape.

He sensed her looking at him as he continued his conversation and smiled at her. Jamie was now asking questions and Beth, just as Katharine had predicted, was looking at Stephen with complete adoration.

Jamie whispered to Katharine, as they got into the station wagon. "I *really* like him, Aunt Katharine. Are you going to marry him?"

Katharine whispered back, "It's too soon to say, Jamie, but I like him, too."

"What's all this whispering?" Stephen demanded. "I was always taught it was rude to whisper in front of people—especially those who are dying to know what you are talking about."

"I just asked Aunt Katharine . . ."

"Shush, Jamie," and Katharine's face began to redden.

Stephen noticed and said, "Let the young man have the floor."

"Well, all I said was . . ." and Jamie turned to grin at his aunt, ". . . are you two going to get married?"

Stephen leaned down and whispered something to Jamie, who beamed and said, "I promise I won't tell!" The two of them laughed and Beth was let in on the secret, too. Her large brown eyes opened wide and she began to smile, jumping up and down in her seat.

"I feel completely left out of this conversation,"

Katharine said, with mock disgust. "It's so impolite."

In unison, they all yelled out, "Sorrrry," as Stephen drove swiftly down Connecticut Avenue to the National Zoological Park. Once inside, the children ran on ahead and Katharine and Stephen walked hand in hand, watching them shriek with delight as they saw the various animals.

"You were right—I really do love them. They are lovely children," Stephen said admiringly. "How many do you want?"

Katharine smiled and said, "Well, when I get married I hope to have two just as wonderful as Beth and Jamie."

"And when do you think that will be," Stephen said looking at her with an inquiring, half-amused look.

"Your lawyer's mind working again?" Katharine walked a few steps away from him, but he quickly caught up with her.

"Not my lawyer's mind—just a mind that tells me I'm in love with you, Katie." He bent down and kissed her and Katharine put her arms around him, standing on her toes. Her sneakers made her even more petite so she reached up and kissed him quickly. But not before the children had seen them and Beth came running back.

"I think Aunt Katharine loves Uncle Stephen!" she said in singsong rhythm.

Jamie clapped his hands and exclaimed, "I knew it, I knew it!" His blonde hair and enormous brown eyes danced as he ran up to them. Jamie had always touched a sensitive chord in Katharine's heart. There was something so delightfully innocent and vulnerable about him. Beth always seemed very sure of herself, as if she were the older child. Katharine did not love Beth less, but Jamie spoke to something deep inside of Katharine . . .

The two children insisted they visit the giraffe compound and Stephen bought some food to feed them. Jamie gave some to Katharine and as she reached out her hand the lofty creature leaned his long neck down and licked her on the face. Stephen caught her distasteful look with his camera and they all laughed.

The hours went by far too quickly for them all and Stephen realized it was time for them to be heading home for the barbecue that Ellen and Jim were preparing. They all sang in the car and played games. Katharine thought what a remarkable afternoon it had been—a remarkable morning, too, spent with the man she loved. She gazed at Stephen's strong profile as he concentrated on the road. He looked back at her and grinned saying, "Hi, giraffe lady. What's it like to be kissed by the tallest quadruped in the world?"

Katharine wrinkled her nose. "Smelly—he definitely needed breath mints!"

Stephen and the children all laughed. He looked back at Katharine and their eyes seemed to speak volumes to each other in the private world of their love.

Chapter Eight

Katharine awakened early Sunday morning and looked over at the alarm clock which was due to send forth its earth-shattering sound in a few minutes. She leaned over and shut it off before it could invade her peaceful, happy thoughts.

Yesterday had been phenomenal. Stephen had made a great hit, not only with the children but also with Ellen and Jim. Ellen had taken her aside and said how much she approved of Stephen.

"He's so natural. I imagined I would feel very awkward around him. My house is hardly competition for the Douglass estate."

Ellen had refused to move from the white clapboard home when Jim had been promoted to colonel even though they could have afforded a larger house. Ellen chose to stay and add on a couple of rooms. Katharine thought of the way her sister had made that house a real home. Family antiques, additions bought at garage sales, and well-chosen accent pieces had added a warmth that made any visitor feel welcome.

Katharine looked around her bedroom. A pile of wallpaper selected after a great deal of consideration, and a bolt of beautiful fabric still sat in a corner waiting to be used. Ellen had promised her she would come over this next week and start helping her decorate. Katharine got out of bed, crossing the room to the fabric and the wallpaper, and put them up to the wall and windows. A feeling of wanting to get started immediately came over her as she put on her robe and brushed her hair.

Then she was brought back to what was happening that day—she was meeting Stephen's mother. He was picking her up at 10 A.M. and driving to the church near the Douglass estate, where Mrs. Douglass would be waiting for them.

A sigh escaped Katharine as she looked critically in the dressing table mirror. She had just over an hour to have breakfast and dress. Katharine remembered the dress she had bought for the occasion. Opening her closet door, she saw it hanging there and decided once more that she had made a good choice. Designed by Bill Blass, its soft lines and pleated skirt were very feminine: the pale lilac silk draped beautifully over her supple figure as she held it against her. The dress gave her a feeling of confidence. She hung it back in the closet and went downstairs to make herself a quick breakfast. Singing to herself, she began to excitedly anticipate another day spent with Stephen.

When he rang the bell at 10 A.M. Katharine was waiting in the living room. Hastily she glanced in the hall mirror and saw that the new pale cream, tricorn straw hat with its fine veil was perched charmingly over her golden hair. Opening the door with a flourish she said, "Isn't it a beautiful day?"

Stephen stood at the top step, holding her at arm's length. He said admiringly, "You look absolutely fantastic!" Kissing her longingly, he then noticed again how lovely she was.

Katharine felt as if she could never, ever feel more wonderful—even the thought of the imposing Mrs. Douglass could not change her mood.

In the station wagon, pacing back and forth, was Blarney, eager to be on his way to the country.

"He always loves to go down to Virginia and run in the fields." Stephen took a quick look at Katharine's attire again. "We'll probably go riding after lunch, so perhaps you should bring some jeans with you. That dress is hardly suitable for roughing it," he said still gazing at Katharine.

"I foresaw there might be a need for jeans and I have them right here." Katharine picked up a large tote bag that had been packed with everything she might require for her day in Virginia.

"Fine," Stephen said and shut her front door. "We're off then."

The Sunday streets of Georgetown were quiet as they wended their way to the Key Bridge, which crossed the Potomac into Virginia.

"Mother said she is looking forward to meeting you when I called her last night."

Katharine smiled and nodded. "I'm anxious to meet her."

Stephen laughed.

"Anxious seems to be the right word!" He put his hand in hers. "I detect beneath that beautiful calm exterior there are definitely apprehensive thoughts, Katie."

"I can't fool you, can I?"

"No. You are an open book as far as I'm concerned."

"You mean the composed, assured person I have striven for years to present to my public doesn't deceive you for a minute?"

He shook his head. "No. I know how deeply you feel about everything. Just know Mother will not devour you. She comes across as being rather foreboding to some people, but I know her, too, remember. She has her vulnerable spots."

Katharine watched the countryside of Virginia begin to appear. The white picket fences and the rolling green hills—some with vigorous prancing horses—relaxed her as she sat close to Stephen. He leaned over and kissed her on the ear, saying softly, "It won't be long before we come to our church."

When the "Warrenton" sign came into view, Katharine knew that in just a few minutes she would be meeting Mrs. Douglass. Stephen drove down a narrow country lane and there, ahead of them, was a perfect example of an eighteenth-century red brick church. Set among towering trees, its graceful lines had been welcoming worshipers for over two hundred years.

Stephen noted that his mother had already arrived—her limousine was parked nearby. After making sure the windows of the station wagon were open enough for Blarney to get some air, Stephen and Katharine made their way up the steps to the church's entrance, his arm around her shoulders.

The cool, inviting interior calmed Katharine. Painted completely in white, with striking mahogany wood making a glowing accent, the church was at once welcoming and worshipful. Stephen escorted Katharine to the Douglass family pew and bent down to kiss his mother, already seated there.

Dressed in a striking black straw picture hat, which emphasized her black and white silk patterned dress, she patted the seat beside her—indicating Stephen should sit next to her. He looked at Katharine for a second, as if asking her understanding and she sat the other side of him. Leaning across Stephen, Mrs. Douglass extended a white gloved hand and shook Katharine's hand, saying, "Welcome to our church, Miss Hayes. Maggie has told me so much about you."

Katharine was completely taken aback. The organist began to play the introduction to the opening hymn and the congregation rose to sing the first verse. Katharine found it difficult to concentrate, her thoughts still with Mrs. Douglass' greeting. "They must have had a great time talking about me," Katharine mused, remembering the iciness of Stephen's secretary.

By the time the minister rose to deliver the sermon, Katharine had composed herself and now listened intently to his message. He spoke on the parable of the talents.

"Our talents are gifts given to us by God," the minister's voice rang out through the nave. "We must use them or they will be lost. We are all gifted, some have more talents than others, but *all* are important. Our world needs these gifts.

We must reach out with our love, caring , intelligence, and skills. We cannot sit back and say that our talents are not needed. Look around you. We have the power, through Jesus Christ, to touch human pain and misery around the world, but we must begin in our own neighborhood."

Stephen turned to look at Katharine and smiled—she knew instinctively he was thinking of the youth center. She returned his smile. Mrs. Douglass fidgeted for a moment and made it clear that they should be concentrating on the minister's words.

Katharine settled back in her seat and listened more intently.

"Years ago, William Temple said, 'The church is the only institution in the world which exists primarily for those outside of itself.' Let us never forget this.

"Jesus loves this world. He died on a cross for you and me. If we accept this gift then we must in turn obey Him and use our talents for Him.

"We sit here this morning in comparative comfort, with the knowledge that we are loved by Almighty God. Realizing this, we show Jesus Christ's love by reaching out to others. Loving them as He has loved us."

Katharine's thoughts turned once more to Mrs. Douglass. Katharine prayed silently, asking the Lord to take away any resentment toward Stephen's mother—no matter how she might treat her that day.

The congregation rose to sing the recessional hymn and at the closing "Amen," Mrs. Douglass indicated it was time for them to leave. Outside, the minister greeted them and Stephen introduced Katharine to him.

"Why, I have seen your excellent reports on the news, Miss Hayes. My prayers go with you— you are helping the needs of others in this area." He smiled at Katharine and added, "Using your talents well, Miss Hayes."

Katharine thanked him and walked on a few steps behind Mrs. Douglass, who was being greeted by many of her fellow believers.

"Let's slip away," Stephen said quietly. "I want to show you a little of our countryside before lunch."

Katharine looked toward Mrs. Douglass questioningly.

"Mother is fine. We'll meet her back at the house."

The matriarch got into her chauffeured limousine and drove off, waving regally to several people—looking for all the world like a queen departing from her subjects.

"I'm going to take you the back way to 'Kingsridge,' " Stephen said animatedly. "It's the way I used to like to go when I was a boy. My brother

Rick and I loved to explore and make up all kinds of dangerous adventures."

Stephen took on a completely different demeanor as he began to reminisce about his childhood. He turned into a driveway which led to "Kingsridge" and proceeded to drive through some rough countryside.

"Rick and I called this our domain. The rest of the family always came in via the front gates—dignified and proper—but we, if we could, preferred the more adventurous way."

He parked the station wagon on the brow of the hill and indicated that he would like Katharine to get out. Blarney went chasing off and Stephen said the dog would make his own way to the house.

Katharine and Stephen walked a few steps to where there was the most beautiful scene, which commanded a view of the whole valley. Small villages could be seen in the distance. Sheep grazed in the fields below. The whole panorama was one of peace and Katharine thought this was one of the most beautiful landscapes she had ever beheld.

"Rick and I would sit here and discuss our futures. We wondered who lived beyond our land. What were their dreams, their hopes, and fears? It was here that one day, all on my own I gave my life over to the Lord." Stephen's eyes misted over at the memory and Katharine, holding his hand, remembered the day when she had had the same experience. It had been during a service at the family church in Connecticut.

"How old were you, Stephen?"

"I had just turned eighteen and I knew then that whatever I would have to face—I would not be alone. Katie, I could never have accomplished anything without Him."

Katharine looked down once more at the valley. She thought of all the Lord had meant to her as she had embarked out into an often bewildering and frightening world.

"I was seventeen when I asked Jesus Christ into my life. I'm so thankful I made that decision." She thought for a moment. "Like you, I know I could never have faced what I have encountered these last few years without the knowledge that wherever I am, He is with me."

Stephen smiled. "Yes, I only wish Rick had that same certainty. I'm looking forward to his coming home and being able to spend some time with him."

Katharine removed her straw hat and shook out her hair. "It's strange how we can be so close as children and then quite suddenly, everything changes. I'm glad I still have a close relationship with Ellen."

Stephen looked down at her, with the summer

breeze now fanning her golden hair and causing her silk dress to ripple. "May we never know what it is to have our relationship changed. I mean it, Katie. You have brought such joy into my life. I couldn't bear to think we would ever go our separate ways."

Suddenly they were in each other's arms, in a world all their own, the valley below them making a welcome retreat from the rest of civilization. Katharine felt his mouth searching hers and she kissed him back with a passion that seemed to consume her.

Minutes went by and they clung to each other, then, regretfully, they returned to the station wagon realizing Mrs. Douglass would be awaiting them for lunch. Katharine hastily touched up her makeup. Stephen laughed at her attempts as he drove the station wagon swiftly and expertly through the winding driveway, that finally led to the back of his family home.

"This is 'Kingsridge.' Welcome, Katie!"

She looked up at the gracious, white, Southern-style mansion, set among sweeping lawns, that overlooked the valley. Horses and sheep roamed the rolling acres of lush green grass. It was captivatingly beautiful. A veranda, furnished with white wicker furniture and masses of ferns, swept right across the imposing house. Katharine noted that buffet tables were already set for luncheon, as were a small table and chairs on the lawn.

Mrs. Douglass' voice could be heard, calling Stephen into the house. He and Katharine walked up the steps to the veranda and into the lofty hallway of the house. Silhouetted against the sunlight, Mrs. Douglass asked rather impatiently, "Now, why did you bring Miss Hayes around the back, Stephen? Surely you know that our guests should enter our home through the front door?"

"I was just showing Katharine our countryside, Mother."

"It is so beautiful, Mrs. Douglass," Katharine said.

"Well, thank you. Mr. Douglass first saw the site for this house many years ago and when he showed it to me I knew it would be the perfect place to build 'Kingsridge.' " Mrs. Douglass stopped her reminiscing and said, "I'm sure you would like to freshen up before lunch, Miss Hayes. The maid will take you upstairs."

Katharine was led up the grand, sweeping staircase to an ornately furnished guest room. She thanked the maid and went over to a mirror, looking thoughtfully at herself. The breeze had swept her hair away from her face, leaving a golden frame around her perfectly formed bone structure. Her high cheekbones were highlighted by a glow that the previous moments with Stephen had accentuated. Katharine smiled as she remembered. She still felt his arms around her and his lips pressing down on hers. A gong sounding in the hall downstairs interrupted her thoughts—hastily she brushed her hair and ran her hands over the shimmering silk dress.

Stephen was waiting for her in the hall and escorted her out onto the veranda, where Mrs. Douglass was giving last-minute instructions to the servants.

"Come, Miss Hayes, please help yourself to whatever you care for. There is some pate to start with or cold vichyssoise, or perhaps you would prefer melon?"

Katharine thanked Mrs. Douglass and selected some of the cold soup. Remarkably, she felt quite hungry, in spite of the tension she had been feeling.

Seated at the table on the lawn, Stephen took over the conversation, realizing it was a rather difficult time for Katharine. Mrs. Douglass seemed distant, as if she were meeting someone she had never heard of, or wanted to hear of, but was purely being polite because of the situation in which she found herself.

After the first course, Mrs. Douglass seemed a little more at ease. "I was very interested in the sermon this morning. Weren't you, Stephen?"

"Yes, Mother. It confirmed once more the responsibility we all have to use our talents wisely. Speaking of talents, have you heard from Rick? He was supposed to call and let me know the exact day he would be arriving from California."

Mrs. Douglass drew herself up and sighed, quite audibly. "Yes, he called last night and said he plans to arrive next Friday. I trust he doesn't bring along any of his wild friends." She touched the corner of her mouth with her napkin and shook it out before replacing it on her lap, as if wanting to remove any thought of having to entertain such people.

Katharine volunteered, "I have read that he has changed considerably in the last few months. That his music is not as..." She caught the incredulous look that Mrs. Douglass had cast her way and paused.

"Really?" There was dead silence. "I certainly trust his appearance has changed."

"He's volunteered to help us at the inner-city youth center, Mother." Stephen watched as his mother appeared not to know what he was talking about. "Now come, Mother, last week we had a long conversation about Katharine's idea for a youth center and Rick giving a concert."

"You probably did, dear Stephen, but I do have so many important matters to attend to." She turned to look at Katharine, as if analyzing this

beautiful media person that her son had somehow become entangled with. "A noble thought,
but one wonders if it would be appreciated or
whether it would work. One can always send
money to these causes, can't one?" She rose from
her chair and walked back up to the veranda.
"Perhaps dessert might tempt you, Miss Hayes?"

A feeling of anger had welled up inside Katharine and as she walked to the veranda she felt
she was being patronized. She longed to be able
to express her feelings, but Stephen winked at
her, as if to say, "Consider the source...I'll talk
to her later."

Katharine remembered the minister's words
of that morning. "Please, Lord, let me really love
this woman," Katharine prayed silently.

They finished their dessert and Stephen told
his mother that he was going to take Katharine
riding. Mrs. Douglass informed them she would
be resting, as more guests would be arriving for
dinner. Her eyes met Katharine's. They seemed
to taunt her. "Some of my favorite people are
coming," she said, walking very erectly toward
the house.

"Why don't you change?" Stephen said quietly
to Katharine, giving her hand an assuring
squeeze.

Katharine ran up the stairs to the guest room
and quickly changed into her jeans, emerging

just as Mrs. Douglass was reaching the top of the stairs. She looked Katharine up and down and murmured something about not having the correct riding attire, then walked on to her bedroom and ceremoniously closed the door.

"Remember the minister's words," Katharine told herself again. "I will not let her get me down, but Lord, *please*, give me Your love for her. I'm finding it more and more difficult on my own."

Stephen had changed and because Katharine had not brought the "correct attire" had thoughtfully worn jeans, too. Katharine ran down the stairs to him and he took her hand and led her out to the stables. A magnificent chestnut horse had been saddled for her by the groom and she mounted the gorgeous creature, who was anxious to be off. She reined him in and waited for Stephen, who was now astride a splendid black horse.

They rode out of the courtyard, with Blarney trotting along beside them. He quickly ran off in search of rabbits, his coat gleaming in the sunlight.

"Happiness is chasing, but never catching, anything." Stephen laughed, watching his dog's dedicated, but futile, search.

They rode on, up through the hills until they came to the ridge, where Stephen had taken

Katharine earlier that day. Dismounting, they tied their horses to some branches and sat down, once more looking at the magnificent scene that stretched endlessly before them.

"I'm sorry Mother is proving to be such a pill. Please give her time. She is a person who makes up her mind about something and is not easily changed. The media have always been an anathema to her and she thinks everyone connected to it is suspect."

"I must say she doesn't hide her feelings," Katharine said wryly.

"No. Forthrightness, according to her, is next to godliness. Katie, don't let this spoil our time together. She is Old World Virginia and changes do not come easily to her. I intend to tell her what I think of her behavior, however."

"I'm still having a wonderful time, just being here with you, Stephen."

He took her face gently in his hands and bent down and kissed her. "Oh, Katie, you fill my days with new meaning."

He put his arm around her shoulder and they sat silently, lost in the thought of their nearness.

"Until you came into my life, I did not realize how lonely I was. Oh, I had plenty to do every day, so many decisions to make, working where I believe I can do something to change circumstances in this country. But, when I went home each night and shut that front door, there was no one to share my day with me. I still go home to an empty house, but now I know that only three streets away, in a quaint little red brick house, lives a lady I have fallen in love with and who understands and cares."

Katharine looked at him, tears in her eyes. "Funny, I was only thinking that last night. When I got into bed and put out the light, I thought of you—not too far away—and my world was no longer just filled with ambitions, but with a love that seems to completely encompass my every thought."

She looked down quickly and traced her fingers through the cool grass.

Stephen began to whisper, " 'In Love, if Love be Love, if Love be ours'..."

Katharine gazed deeply into his eyes. "No 'ifs'...remember?" she said softly.

"I remember." Stephen pulled her toward him and all the strivings and tensions of the world were forgotten—they were only conscious of their love.

Chapter Nine

❧

The house seemed cramped and small after visiting the Douglass estate, but Katharine welcomed the coziness of her Georgetown home. True, the mansion was beautiful but uppermost in her mind was the cold reception she had received from Stephen's mother. It seemed to spread a pall on an otherwise glorious day with Stephen.

Katharine took a long look at herself in the mirror, as she cleansed her face and prepared for bed. She was not of the right set for Mrs. Douglass. Her "favorite people" had turned out to definitely be from the upper crust of Virginian society, and when these guests had arrived for dinner Mrs. Douglass had virtually ignored Katharine.

Stephen introduced her to the people, but his mother chose to walk right past Katharine, deep in conversation. The big surprise of the evening was that Maggie had been invited and had

131

occupied much of Mrs. Douglass' attention.

Maggie looked stunning. Her hair, usually swept up in a businesslike knot, had been brushed down on her shoulders, and the raven hair against a figure-hugging cream silk dress had made a very glamorous effect. Stephen, sensing Katharine's uneasiness, had tried to stay by her side as much as possible, but Maggie had succeeded in monopolizing him most of the evening.

There was a nagging thought that kept recurring. How long would Stephen feel that his relationship with Katharine transcended any of his mother's reticence to accept her? Maggie apparently was favored by Mrs. Douglass. The Douglass' had always been close-knit, almost jealous of any outside influence. Stephen's father had dominated family policy; now his mother had taken on the mantle. Could it be that she favored Maggie? After all, Maggie's father had been a senator. Or was she merely being used to distract Stephen?

Katharine sat on the edge of her bed and automatically kicked off her slippers. "Stephen is strong," she thought. "He's influenced by his mother, but ultimately, it seems, whatever decisions have to be made are his and his alone."

She flung back the white, frilly eyelet covers and got into bed. This week, she remembered,

Ellen was coming to help supervise the transformation of this little house. Smoothing the pillow, Katharine leaned over and turned out the bedside light and sank thankfully back into the comfort of her bed.

There was still another week of anchoring before Sally Denton would come back to the studio, which meant Katharine must give her full attention to her career. Stephen had occupied so much of her time—was it to the detriment of her career? She brushed these thoughts aside. He was the most important thing that had happened in her life. Analyzing herself as she lay there in the dark, Katharine knew she was only using the importance of her career as a defense mechanism.

She thought of him again, only three streets away, and she remembered his words, high on the hill at "Kingsridge": "You have brought such joy into my life...I couldn't bear to think we would ever go our separate ways..."

Katharine turned her face into the softness of the pillow and a tear trickled down her cheek. The hurt she still felt from Mrs. Douglass' behavior now seemed to obliterate the sureness Katharine had felt of Stephen's love.

"Lord, I do love him. But I sense that his love may change for me...."

●　　　●　　　●

There had been so much happening in the world, the news department was having difficulty knowing just what to feature. Alan Holt had gone over the latest events with Katharine and together they had tried to keep up with what was coming in over the wire. There were only thirty minutes to go before news time and still the script was not finalized.

Alan began to slash some items, knowing they would have to go, even though they were important.

"Keep the 'People' segment in and we can throw it out if there's any more late-breaking news."

"Right, Alan." Katharine was thankful he had not been his usual abrasive self. The knowledge that the network executives were still around helped tremendously. Alan's personality had taken a complete turn with Katharine and the whole news staff was glad for the respite.

It was now two minutes before air time and Katharine's microphone was being hooked up. Hastily she scanned her script once more and hoped the TelePrompter girl had made all the last-minute changes. The signal was given and WNSC News was on the air.

Katharine masterfully coped with reading the news. There had been many calls and letters coming into the station from viewers saying how much they appreciated her handling of the anchor position. Glancing at the studio clock during a commercial, Katharine saw that there were only five more minutes to go. Stephen was attending a party at the British embassy and was not sure if he would be able to see her. She wondered if Maggie had been able to wangle an invitation. That morning in Julia Simpson's column she intimated that Stephen was seeing his secretary socially since his station wagon had been seen outside Maggie's apartment building.

Katharine rationalized that there was nothing unusual about that—Stephen probably had dropped off some tapes for her to type. Nevertheless, it had bothered Katharine. Stephen had told her that Washington parties always end at 11 P.M. but he was often caught up afterward with one of the guests telling him how to solve the world's problems.

She caught herself just in time—her thoughts had been wandering. The floor manager gave her the signal that she was half a minute from going back on the air and a bulletin was being handed to her.

"I have just been notified of a kidnapping in Bethesda," she said calmly. "On your screen you will be seeing the photograph of a little boy who was last seen in the Bethesda Shopping Mall this evening at 7:30 P.M."

Katharine looked at the monitor and was stunned... Jamie, her nephew, was looking right at her. She broke out in a cold sweat, but managed to continue.

"His name is Jamie Bartlett, and he is seven years old." Katharine felt her throat constrict as she read on. "When last seen he was wearing blue jeans and a striped navy and white shirt. His sister told the police they were approached by a man, approximately six feet tall with dark hair, wearing a blue T-shirt and old beige pants. Bethesda police ask that anyone who knows the whereabouts of Jamie Bartlett, or having any knowledge of the incident, please contact them immediately at the number now on your screen."

She managed to keep calm until the news program went off the air, then an agonized cry escaped that seemed to come from deep within her.

"He's my nephew...!" The anguished cry filled the studio and in a daze, Katharine unhooked her microphone and ran out to her dressing room. Picking up her handbag, she rushed past people in the hallway—many of them wanting to help her—and ran out to her car. The engine would not start at first, then finally it did and she backed out of her parking stall and drove swiftly to the exit, almost colliding with a car which was turning in.

Katharine saw that it was Stephen, who was shouting something to her. She rolled down her window and heard him say, "Park your car. We'll go in mine."

Obediently, she backed up and after parking, ran to get in Stephen's station wagon.

"I heard it on the radio on my way over here." Stephen put his arm around Katharine and held her close. "We'll find him, Katharine. Hang in there."

Stephen drove swiftly on the parkway to Bethesda, the radio giving information about Jamie's kidnapping. Katharine seemed to freeze inside. It could not be happening. They would find that he was safe in his bed when they got to the house. Thoughts swirled—fears were mounting and a sick, ashen feeling had taken hold of her. The thought of Jamie being in the possession of some deranged person terrified her. She wanted to pray, but no words came. She wanted to cry, but there were no tears. Then she felt Stephen's comforting hand in hers.

"Katharine, we have to remember that wherever Jamie is he's with our Lord. Right at this very minute He knows where the boy is."

A whisper came from the anguished Katharine. "I know. I know...but Stephen, I'm terrified."

They passed the shopping mall where Jamie

was last seen, situated just a short distance from his home—police cars and dogs were evident. Katharine prayed silently that she might be able to console Ellen.

Stephen turned down the street leading to the Bartlett home and they were immediately greeted with a barrage of police and reporters. Many recognized Katharine and Stephen and wanted to know more details. They had none and could only say they would let them know anything they learned later.

They pushed their way up to the front door, which was ajar as Katharine led Stephen into the living room. Ellen was sitting staring into space, not aware that Katharine had arrived. Beth was huddled close to her. When she saw Katharine and Stephen the girl leaped up and ran to them crying, "Please help find Jamie!" The tears were rolling down her face. "I love him, Aunt Katharine—Uncle Stephen!"

Katharine kneeled and hugged Beth to her. "We'll find him, Beth." Katharine looked over at Ellen who still sat, seemingly in a trance.

Stephen went over and sat beside her. "Ellen, everything is being done that can possibly be done. The police have every available man working to find Jamie."

Ellen turned to look at him and tried to say, "Thank you," but no words came. Katharine, leading Beth by the hand, walked over to Ellen and kissed her.

"Where's Jim, Ellen?"

Ellen shook her head, as if she had no idea. "Daddy's away, Aunt Katharine. He left this morning."

Katharine looked at Stephen, who walked over to the telephone and called the Pentagon. After a few minutes' conversation, he came back to Ellen and said, "Jim has already been informed and is on his way home. He will be here by six tomorrow morning."

Ellen put her hand out to Stephen and suddenly, the tears she had not been able to express, poured down her stricken face. Katharine's arms were around her and she felt Stephen's hand in hers. Beth climbed up on her mother's lap and said, trying to comfort her, "Daddy's coming home, Mommy. You'll see, Jamie will be home soon, too."

The feeling of love that enveloped Ellen began to break through the horror of it all. She said, haltingly, "It all happened so quickly. Jamie was taking Beth to get ice cream, while I finished paying for some shirts I had bought him." Ellen leaned forward, her head in her hands. "If only I hadn't said they could go, but had made them wait until I could go with them..."

"No recriminations, Ellen," Stephen said comfortingly. "Try to remember if you had seen anyone following you around."

Ellen said dazedly, "No, I can't remember anything like that. We were just doing some shopping and I had told the children it was time to go home, that it was getting near their bedtime." She put her hands up to her face, "Jamie should be in bed . . . it's dark out there and I don't know where he is . . ." She cried, "Please, God, help him . . ."

Tears were in Katharine's eyes as she said softly, "*He* is with him, Ellen. We've got to believe that."

Stephen went out to the front door and was deep in conversation with the police sergeant. They both walked back into the room and Sergeant Walker asked if he might question Beth again. Ellen nodded and told Beth to help the policeman. "Try to remember *everything*, Beth," she whispered.

The sergeant sat down beside Beth and said with understanding, "I know we have gone all over it before, Beth, but please tell me again what happened."

Beth looked up into his face and began to describe the man once more. "He asked Jamie to help him find the pet shop. Jamie said he would be back in a minute and for me to pay for the ice cream."

"Did you see him walk off with the man?" Sergeant Walker asked gently.

"Yes, Jamie was laughing. I heard the man saying something about wanting to buy a puppy and perhaps Jamie could help him pick one out. I wanted to go, too, but Jamie left me with the money for the ice cream." Beth's little face began to crumple and she cried. "I wish I had gone with him."

Sergeant Walker assured her that they were going to find Jamie and that he would not question her anymore tonight. He told Stephen confidentially that the people who ran the pet shop had not seen anyone come into the store answering Jamie's or the man's description. The boy's jacket had been found in the parking lot, as if it had dropped when he got into a car. The sergeant thanked Ellen and everyone, then said he would be outside if they needed him.

Katharine asked Stephen if they could stay with Ellen for the night and when she started to protest, Stephen said, "Ellen, we insist. We are not leaving until Jim gets back."

In the kitchen, Katharine made some coffee for them all. Beth refused to go to bed, but curled up on her mother's lap and fell asleep. They sat around the table, holding hands and praying—interrupted constantly by the telephone. Reporters, wire services, neighbors, friends, all wanting to know if there was any more news.

"I would like to be able to take the phone off the hook, but I know I can't," Ellen said with exasperation. "The police are having the line tapped and each call could be the kidnapper asking for a ransom."

It rang once more and Katharine went over to answer it. "Mother! How did you hear? We weren't going to worry you until the morning."

"Your father heard it on the Cable News Network and called me. He said they mentioned that Jim worked at the Pentagon." Sarah Hayes' voice broke. "We're coming down, Katharine. First thing tomorrow."

The kidnapping was now of national importance. The fact that Jamie's father worked at the Pentagon had made it take on an even more sinister tone. The premise that the kidnapper could be a terrorist was not being ruled out.

A knock at the front door, heralding the F.B.I. who asked that they be given a room in which to set up their surveillance equipment, made the whole incident seem even more nightmarish.

Katharine's nerves were taut, yet she felt controlled and capable of being able to help her sister.

"Thank You, Lord. I know You are with us."

Ellen finally agreed to try to sleep in their family room on the sofa with Beth. Stephen pushed two armchairs together and he and Katharine sat in them—the lonely, aching night's vigil ahead . . .

Katharine put her head on his shoulder and felt the strength and concern of this man she had grown to love. He took her hand and put it to his lips and whispered, "Everything that's possible is being done for Jamie, Katie. We've got to keep praying and believing God will answer."

Almost as if she were praying to herself, she said softly, "Lord, I believe. Help thou mine unbelief."

The light shining in from the hall fell on Jamie's baseball bat—a silent reminder of the little boy who was lost in the abyss of this terrifying night. Katharine thought again of his room upstairs—unoccupied, empty, waiting for his return . . . .

Chapter Ten

The telephone had continued to ring late into the night. The police had received a call from a man who remembered seeing a boy, answering Jamie's description, being pushed into a green van. He had thought it was the child's father who was angry with him about someing. The caller had run after the vehicle with Jamie's jacket after seeing it fall to the ground. He left it there, thinking they might come back for it. A good description of the kidnapper and the van had been given to the police. The caller had remembered the first three letters of the license plate. It was a very positive, hopeful lead.

Jim arrived home and Ellen and Beth ran into his welcome arms. Ellen now felt stronger with her husband by her side. They had thanked Stephen for all he had done and Katharine was hugged by a grateful Jim.

"Thank God you were both here."

Taking them both aside while Ellen was preoccupied with a neighbor, Jim confided that at the Pentagon there was a great sense of apprehension about the kidnapping.

"They have been receiving some recorded messages by phone. The caller is threatening to kill Jamie unless the man who was arrested last week for planting an incendiary device in the Capitol is released." He paused for a minute, trying to control his voice. "We can't give in to terrorism, but... he's my son. He's so *young!*" There was a haunted, fearful expression in his eyes. The tall, disciplined soldier quickly wiped away the tears that had formed as Ellen returned to them.

Katharine was devastated and turned away from Ellen so that the anguish on her face would not be seen. The thought of Jamie being harmed in any way had made the night horrendous—now to know that the kidnapper was threatening to kill him. She felt Stephen's hand on her shoulder and she swung around to him and buried her head in his chest.

Stephen whispered, "Katharine, ask God for His courage." His silence spoke deeply of his love and concern for her. It was a comfort.

"I know."

Katharine felt the extent of her weariness envelop her. "We must go, now that Jim is here. Mother and Dad will be arriving soon. I know you have a busy day ahead of you at the Hill."

Stephen glanced at his watch. "I have exactly two hours to get home, shave, shower, and get to the Senate. We're in a heated debate today. I have proposed a bill for emergency food and medical assistance to the legitimately needy people. It has been stymied by interdepartmental haggling but I believe the appropriate funds will be forthcoming."

He assured Ellen and Jim he would continue to do all he could for Jamie.

Katharine and Stephen were greeted by the press and television cameras as soon as they emerged from the house. Both of them made an impassioned plea that the kidnapper would return Jamie safely to his parents. Katharine's WNSC mini-cam crew videoed a special interview, in which she told the viewers she would be with them on the eleven o'clock news with the latest update. Her face wore the gaunt look of someone suffering indescribable pain, but her eyes expressed hope.

"I'm asking all our viewers to pray for Jamie and his abductor. There is no more powerful force than prayer."

Stephen helped her into his station wagon saying, "That was superb, Katharine. People are really going to respond."

He drove swiftly down the parkway and

dropped Katharine off at her house. "Know I'm thinking of you all day. Call my office if you need me. Maggie can get a message to me on the floor of the Senate."

In spite of her feelings of exhaustion and grief, Katharine smiled wryly. "But will she?" Her questioning look was met with a playful tap on her nose as Stephen bent to kiss her.

"I'll fire her if she doesn't."

"Is that a threat or a promise?" Katharine called over her shoulder, while putting her key in the door. Stephen just grinned and waved and drove off down the street.

Katharine picked up the *Times* from the top step and scanned the headlines as she entered the house. Jamie's kidnapping was front page news and the ominous words seemed to drive home even more the terrifying events that had taken place. From Jamie's photograph, his innocent, enormous eyes looked up at her as if saying, "Help me, Aunt Katharine."

Closing the door, Katharine made for the stairs and her bedroom—reading the newspaper as she went. Jamie's story was continued on page twelve and she folded it to that page. Hastily, she changed into her robe, then got into bed and went on reading the details. Tears were making the print blur and she reached for a Kleenex.

Julia Simpson's column was on the same page

and Katharine thought how empty all the gossip seemed that the woman spread around Washington, especially compared to Jamie's kidnapping. Katharine glanced at the column and noticed that her name was mentioned.

> What does Katharine Hayes think these days of her Senator Stephen Douglass, seen last night with his glamorous secretary Maggie Taylor at the glittering British Embassy party? Ms. Taylor never left his side.
>
> Such devotion seems to imply more than secretarial duties, but then Ms. Hayes is busy over at WNSC each evening, anchoring the news. How very frustrating for her.

Katharine threw the newspaper across the room and it hit the wallpaper and material stacked in the corner, waiting to be used. The pile scattered and rolled across the floor. Exasperated, Katharine thought again about Ellen coming this week to help her decorate—now Jamie's kidnapping made it all seem so unimportant.

She set the alarm clock so that she could have a few hours' sleep before having to go to the studio. Curled up in bed, Katharine felt as if she had not slept for weeks; yet her mind could not stop the tormenting thoughts...Jamie's face kept coming before her, even as she closed her eyes. Then Maggie and Stephen at the British Embassy party taunted her. Irrationally, Katharine wondered why Stephen had not told her that Maggie was with him.

"It was not important enough," she thought. "Jamie had been uppermost in his mind." Yet the thought still nagged at her until finally sleep, blessedly, came to claim her completely for a few hours.

•   •   •

Katharine sat before the mirror in her studio dressing room, reading her Bible. She knew that the only way she would be able to face the cameras that night was with the comfort from God's Word. Others in the studio had often teased Katharine, some quite cuttingly, about her ever-present Bible. Alan was always the most caustic with his remarks, but Katharine had never been deterred from keeping her Bible prominently before her. It was her strength and she knew that many times in her life she would have been lost without its assurances. Connie had often asked questions about Katharine's commitment and genuinely seemed interested in wanting to find answers for her own life.

Tonight, knowing she had no strength of her own, Katharine read the words of David, in his

Psalm 30—"Weeping may endure for a night, but joy cometh in the morning."

"How long will our night be, Lord? I pray that joy will return for all of us...soon."

Her thoughts turned to Ellen. She had telephoned her in the afternoon when the alarm went off, but there was no more news. Katharine had talked with her parents, who were completely devastated. Their grandchildren had become the brightest part of their lives and now for Jamie to be somewhere out there...well, it didn't bear thinking about. Her mother had not been able to continue talking with Katharine and had handed the telephone to her father.

"Dad, I know you can't talk now, but how are things going between the two of you?"

He had paused and then said, "There's hope, Katharine. But it's still as if a wall...keep praying."

"I am, you know that, Dad. I feel as if my whole world right now is being shattered. The people I love are hurting so badly...."

Katharine, realizing the time, closed her Bible and went to answer the knock on her dressing room door.

It was Frank Murray, one of the executives from the network. "I know this is a very difficult day for you, Katharine, but I wanted you to know, once more, how highly we regard your work. The way you handled last night's news and the bulletin about your nephew was masterful."

Katharine thanked him and said that everyone had been so kind. "It's still hard for me to believe that this is actually happening to *my* family. You get so used to dealing with the rest of the world's crises, you begin to feel that you are somehow immune. But, of course, you're not." Her voice broke for a second, but she caught herself and asked him to come in and sit down.

Frank Murray accepted her invitation and sat for a few moments sizing Katharine up once more, then, choosing his words carefully, he said, "We are interested in your reaction to something. I know you can't think about anything else except your nephew right now and I completely understand. But the network would like you to consider substituting for our anchor in New York for six weeks."

Katharine had never been quite so surprised in her life. "Six weeks?" was all she could say.

"Yes, John Webster is taking a leave of absence and we would like to try a woman anchor as a sub for him. Before you say 'No,' let me say that this could lead to a permanent position in New York, which of course would mean national coverage."

Katharine murmured something about being flattered and completely taken aback. The shock of this news, combined with Jamie's kidnapping, made her feel as if what she were hearing was somehow unreal.

Realizing that Katharine was only forty-five minutes from air time, Frank Murray assured her that he did not expect a decision immediately. "I have to go back to New York, otherwise I would have waited, but I wanted to talk to you myself. You would need to be in New York in two weeks..."

She shook his hand as he left and thanked him for his faith in her and his concern. Shutting the door, she leaned against it and closed her eyes.

"Lord, nothing seems real to me at this moment. Help me to make the right decision, but most of all...help us *find* Jamie!" Tears had started to form and she knew she could not submit to them. Instead, she went to the makeup department to ready herself for the news program.

It was so hard when she came to the portion of the news that concerned Jamie. A report had reached the studio that the police had acted on a lead, and they hoped to have some more definite news later. So many people were praying for Jamie, surely God would answer soon...

Katharine returned to her dressing room to

find a message from Stephen, who had been held up at a dinner engagement, but would be at her house at 12:30 A.M. to take her to Ellen's. Wanting to be with her family, Katharine had accepted Stephen's offer to drive her to Bethesda that night. He would leave her there, then return in the morning to bring her back to Georgetown.

Katharine started her car. In a way she welcomed the drive back to her house alone. It would give her time to think and perhaps clear her mind of the conflicting thoughts that now more than ever were possessing her.

New York? Would she want to leave Washington? Frank Murray's offer had really stunned her. If she worked out during those six weeks, would it mean leaving Stephen and only seeing him on an occasional weekend? Leaving her family—the youth center that was just about ready to begin operating? But New York might mean the culmination of her ambition. She turned on the radio and tried to drown out all these questions. A bulletin about Jamie pierced through her bewilderment.

"A man answering the description of the kidnapper has been identified from police files. An update will be given. . ."

A ray of hope went through Katharine and she thanked God that it seemed as if prayers were being answered.

"I'll keep remembering that joy comes in the morning, Lord."

Katharine parked outside her house and ran up the narrow front steps. As she put her key in the door, she noticed the geraniums were drooping once more. "Sometimes I wonder if you are worth all the trouble," she said to herself and went into the house. Putting her keys on the small hall table, she ran down the steps to the kitchen and opened the back door. The watering can was where Stephen had left it the other night—right where someone could trip over it. Katharine smiled and went back in the kitchen to fill it, then walked back up to the front door to water the thirsty plants, bending over to break off some of their dead flowers.

Without warning, an arm came around her neck from behind. A hand clamped over her mouth. For a brief second she thought it was Stephen. Then as the grip on her intensified, she knew that it was not the man she loved. A brutal, guttural voice demanded she stand still.

Katharine felt the point of a knife at her neck. Without hesitating she used a debilitating kick she had learned at a self-defense class, which sent her attacker reeling. Between the watering can clattering down the steps and his effort to retrieve the knife he had dropped, the man was distracted long enough for Katharine to run into the house and slam the front door.

Standing in the hall, she began to shake uncontrollably. Fear had made her throat constrict and she felt as if she were going to choke. Then the horrifying realization hit her—she had left the back door open!

She stumbled down the steps to the kitchen, in time to see the man's frightening face peering in the window. With a leap toward the back door, Katharine flung herself against it and tried to drive the bolt home, but it was too late. The door crashed open, throwing Katharine against the refrigerator and there stood her assailant, the knife gleaming in his hand.

The dark, straggly-haired man looked quickly around the kitchen and ripped the cord from the coffee machine and walked toward Katharine, a menacing look on his face.

Even as she went to defend herself, he twisted her arms behind her and, with the knife between his teeth, he tied her hands so tightly she cried out in pain.

"That's nothing, lady, compared to what's going to happen to you. Not even your big-shot senator can help you now."

He shoved a portion of a dish towel in her mouth and pushed her into a chair. Katharine glanced furtively at the clock on the wall. It was 12:25 A.M. Stephen was due at the house in five minutes. Fearfully, she wondered if she would ever see him again...

Sitting in absolute terror, Katharine looked at the man and suddenly realized who he was! "Approximately six feet tall, with dark straggly hair. Dressed in a blue T-shirt and old beige pants..." The bulletin had described him perfectly.

He was Jamie's kidnapper!

"God, dear God...help me..." Katharine prayed.

Chapter Eleven

The incessant knocking at the door angered the man. Stephen had arrived on time and kept ringing the bell, then alternately knocking. Katharine, terrified that the kidnapper would open the door and harm Stephen, tried to spit out the gag and warn him. The kidnapper pushed it in harder and hissed, "Don't even *think* of making a sound."

He carried her, walking stealthily up the steps and into the living room, throwing Katharine onto the sofa. Walking to the window he tried to see through the curtains who was at the door. With his back to her, Katharine managed to edge her way to the piano. She fell on the keyboard and the discordant sound made Stephen realize she was there.

"Katharine?" he yelled. "What's happened?"

She tried to reach the keyboard again, but the kidnapper angrily pushed her away with such force that she fell to the floor. There was silence and Katharine thought Stephen must have left. She heard a car door close and her heart sank. There was a deathly silence and all she could hear was the heavy breathing of her assailant as he stood over her...waiting and listening. There was no sound of a car driving off.

Could it be that Stephen was still outside? Katharine's heart was beating so loudly, it seemed to drown out any other sound.

The kidnapper left her for a moment to go into the kitchen—checking to see whether anyone had gone around to the back of the house. As soon as he was out of sight, Katharine got to her feet and darted into the hall and made for the front door keys. With her hands still tied behind her back, she managed to pick them up and was returning to the living room—just as the man came up the steps.

"And where do you think you're going?" he said angrily under his breath. He pushed her into the living room and hurled her onto the sofa once again. Katharine was thankful that she had been able to hold onto the keys tightly so they had not jingled. She felt them digging into her hands, but she did not dare move her fingers. Her assailant went to the front door and listened. There was no sound, except passing traffic. Then there were footsteps coming down the street and people's voices. But they walked past the house and he exhaled a sigh of relief.

The man sat in the armchair across from Katharine and leered at her. "Now I have two hostages," he whispered threateningly.

Katharine had a growing awareness that she had seen the man before. She tried to remember where, but the terror she felt and the pain from the keys jabbing into her hand made everything seem unreal. She prayed that somehow this nightmare would end.

The clock on the mantelpiece ticked quietly and the minutes seemed like hours. The man continued to sit looking at her.

"I have watched you many times, Miss Katharine Hayes," he said with a sneer. "Miss Do-Gooder with her fancy senator."

The gag was making her feel ill with breathing becoming more difficult, yet Katharine wished she could ask him what he had done with Jamie. The man got up and walked over to her and bent down, saying, "Think you can change the world with your *charity*? Why don't you talk to your colonel brother-in-law and get him to change the military? That's what needs changing!" The suppressed anger in his voice made him even more frightening and unpredictable.

She thought she heard a noise, but so often the old house creaked and groaned. The man stood

up and listened. There it was again—as if someone was upstairs or on the roof. He quickly ran
out of the room and listened, then crept halfway
up the stairs. Katharine heard subdued voices
outside the living room window. She got up and
ran and with all the strength she had left kicked
the window, shattering the glass. Turning her
back, she hurled the keys outside.

The noise brought the kidnapper running into the room to see what she had done. He lunged
toward her, his arm upraised as he went to
strike her. The front door burst open and there
were two policemen with their guns drawn.

"Hold it right there!" the curt order sounded
through the house. The man dropped his knife
and the officers grabbed him and in seconds had
him handcuffed.

Stephen pushed past them and ran over to
Katharine. "Oh, thank God. I was so afraid we
wouldn't make it in time."

He untied her hands and she flung them
around his neck, tears pouring down her face.
"He's the kidnapper! He knows where Jamie is!"
Katharine managed to shout.

The police immediately began questioning the
man, but he refused to say anything.

"I know I have seen him somewhere before..." Katharine said with exasperation.
"Stephen, can you remember seeing him?"

Stephen looked at the man questioningly, trying to remember where he might have seen him. Then he looked down at the beige pants and saw splotches of paint that the man had obviously tried to remove.

It suddenly registered. "The youth center! Katharine, he was at the youth center painting with us. He was one of the volunteers! Remember?"

Katharine, who had been nursing her bruised mouth, nodded excitedly. "You're right! I remember now, he brushed past and apologized for getting some of the paint on my jeans!" She thought for a second, then exclaimed, "You don't think he could have hidden Jamie at the center, do you?"

Stephen looked at the policemen and they asked where it was located. "We'll get a squad car over there immediately. In the meantime, we'll take your unwelcome visitor to the station and book him. Will you be all right, Miss Hayes?" Katharine assured them she would be, as Stephen went to find something with which to board up the broken window.

The police left with the man, who began to shout obscenities about the military and people connected with it. Katharine was relieved when she heard the police car drive off and she felt Stephen's arms around her once more. He kissed her gently, then went over and boarded up the window. "We don't want any more uninvited guests arriving tonight. I'll get the glass put in tomorrow for you."

Katharine asked that they go over to the old supermarket to see if they had found Jamie. Driving over, Stephen asked, "Are you sure you're all right, Katie? You've had a terrible experience." She nodded and promised him she was all right. Stephen said, "I was so concerned he would harm you before I could get help. Your signal with the piano tipped me off that you were in the house. Plus the watering can and all the spilled water down the steps made me realize there must have been a struggle. The biggest tip-off was when he came and stood by the curtains. I could see his silhouette by the light coming from the hall. I quickly went to the station wagon and closed the door..."

"I heard you. I thought you were going to leave..."

"I called for the police on the car phone and, thank the Lord, they responded so quickly."

"I heard a noise on the roof," Katharine wondered.

"I threw some stones up there, thinking it might distract him."

"It did. It was then that I was able to smash the window and throw out the keys."

Stephen turned down the street which led to the youth center and noticed a blockade. Many police cars had already arrived. He leaned out of the window and identified himself and Katharine to the police. "It's her nephew we think might be being held there."

The policeman contacted his superior on his radio and was told he could let them through. Stephen recognized the District of Columbia chief of police and took Katharine over to him.

"We know the layout of this supermarket well. Perhaps we can help."

The police chief was adamant in not wanting them near the building.

"There may be others holed up inside. The best thing you can do is to draw a diagram of the place—then we'll send in the S.W.A.T. team, if we don't get an answer from anyone."

Hastily, Stephen and Katharine drew a diagram as exact as they could remember and gave it to the police chief.

"Great. This will be very helpful."

They went back to wait in the car. Katharine began to shake again and Stephen held her close to him. "God, keep Jamie safe, if he's there. Help Katharine, dear Father."

Katharine felt as if her whole insides were being torn apart. Her hands ached from the keys digging into them and her wrists and mouth throbbed from the vicious way her assailant had tied and gagged her. But it was her heart that ached the most. Fear, apprehension, and the continuing threat to Jamie made her heart feel as if it was going to break.

Suddenly, they saw some of the S.W.A.T. team run into the supermarket. Then there was dead silence and, for what seemed like an eternity, nothing appeared to be happening. The police chief walked over to them.

"They've checked all the storage rooms and offices. Could there be anywhere else someone could be hiding?"

Katharine thought for a moment, trying to clear her mind. She went to shake her head, then she recalled that there was what looked like a small opening in the ceiling near the back door, that might go to a loft or a storage area over the supermarket. The chief radioed the information to his men.

Another police car arrived and two German shepherd dogs and their handlers entered the building. Once more there was silence. The street was tense.

Even at the late hour, some crowds had gathered to watch and people leaned out of nearby houses, curious to know what could be happening at the old supermarket.

Minutes went by, then Katharine looked at the

back door and she shouted, "It's Jamie! They've found Jamie!"

A policeman was carrying him out, surrounded by several members of the S.W.A.T. team. Katharine and Stephen got out of the car and ran to Jamie.

His little face lit up as he saw them. "Aunt Katharine! Uncle Stephen!" The police handed him over to them and they all hugged. Katharine was whispering, "Thank You, dear Lord. He's safe. Oh, Jamie, Jamie . . ."

The little boy looked tired and very dirty. His mouth was red, from where it had been taped, his blonde hair was tousled and his clothes were creased and torn, but Katharine thought she had never seen a more beautiful sight.

She looked up at Stephen and said, "Joy has come very early this morning. God promised me, Stephen." Tears were coursing down her face as he kissed her tenderly and they held Jamie close.

Katharine was unaware that WNSC's mini-cam crew had arrived and were filming the poignant scene. . . .

Chapter Twelve

Sally Denton came back to the studio a few nights earlier than intended. Katharine's doctor had insisted she take a few days off to recover from her ordeal. In spite of her protests, Alan urged her to take advantage of a brief vacation.

The little townhouse had too many bad memories for Katharine and she was glad to be able to stay out at Bethesda with Ellen and Jim for a while. Jamie appeared not to have suffered too badly from his kidnapping and bounced right back to his usual happy, mischievous self. It was Ellen who could not seem to realize the terrible ordeal was over.

Katharine saw that it would be a long time before her sister could relax whenever Jamie and Beth were away from her.

Much to Katharine's surprise, Stephen's mother had telephoned saying how thankful she was that Katharine had found her nephew. "Stephen has told me so much about Jamie and his sister. Perhaps one day they can come to 'Kingsridge' and enjoy the countryside."

Mrs. Douglass' voice had actually sounded warm and understanding. Katharine had put the telephone down and stood looking at it incredulously for several minutes. What had changed this woman's attitude? Katharine would have to ask Stephen.

He was coming over later to take her to dinner at an old inn tucked away in a picturesque village in Virginia. There was so much she wanted to talk to him about. She had purposely not yet mentioned the New York network offer. Katharine had never felt so torn about anything.

Over lunch she discussed it with her parents, who were very excited for her. Mrs. Hayes had been quick to notice that her daughter was not as thrilled as she should be.

"Is it because of Stephen?" she asked, understanding.

"Yes, Mother. It would mean we would only be able to see each other for an occasional weekend, here and there." Katharine pushed away her plate and said softly, "I really do love him."

"Has he asked you to marry him?" her father asked.

"No, not yet. But he has told me that he loves

me, too. It's just . . ." Katharine did not want to pursue the subject. "It's very obvious to me that Mrs. Douglass does not approve of me. Although I must say, her phone call this morning seemed to indicate a slight thaw." Katharine smiled. "It's strange—I have interviewed so many well-known people and very seldom have I found them as intimidating as she is."

"Perhaps it's because you both love the same man," her mother answered thoughtfully.

Katharine looked at her mother for a moment. "Perhaps. Yes, perhaps you're right, Mother."

Her father said, "If Stephen is the one God has chosen for you, He's going to work the rest out. I must say, I think the Senator is a very special person, Katie. Both your mother and I approve."

Katharine reached for their hands and said, "Now if only my dear parents would realize how much God wants them to forget *their* differences. . . ."

Mrs. Hayes' eyes clouded up and she began to cry. "I'm so ashamed of myself. Little Jamie's kidnapping has made me see how precious every day is together. I don't know where all the hateful thoughts and the things I said ever came from. I have asked the Lord to forgive me." Drying her eyes, she looked over at her husband. "Can *you* ever forgive me?"

Her husband went over and put his arms

around her. "Of course, Sarah. Forgive me for all the heartache I have caused you—and for not being as sensitive to your feelings as I should have been."

Katharine put her hands in theirs. "Two wonderful events in one day. It's almost too much for me to believe. God has answered our prayers and all I can do is praise Him..."

The three of them stood quietly together, their heads bowed.

"Joy cometh in the morning..." seemed to resound through Katharine's whole being.

•   •   •

Stephen arrived at the house in a jubilant mood.

"The Senate passed my bill! I still can't believe it! Even though I hardly had any sleep last night, they said I gave the best speech, the most persuasive speech, I have ever made!" Kissing Katharine, he said, "See how good you are for me?"

She was so happy to see his joy. "I'm so delighted for you, Stephen. I knew you could persuade them."

They drove into the countryside of Virginia, the peacefulness making it hard to believe all that had transpired during the last few days. Katharine was reminded over and over again of

God's goodness to her and her family. But seated beside Stephen, there was still the nagging question of how she would tell him about the New York offer. He was busy pointing out different places that had meant so much to him during his childhood, unaware of the turmoil that was going on in Katharine's mind.

Stephen drove up to the quaint, eighteenth-century inn. The gardens were still a blaze of color, even though it was the end of summer. A few last roses of the season lined the walkway into the low-ceilinged building.

"This is really beautiful, Stephen." Her eyes traveled over the old beams and the rough granite stone walls. Stephen and Katharine were led to a table that overlooked the magnificent landscaped gardens at the back of the inn.

"We'll sit outside after dinner," Stephen suggested. "I ordered a moon, but as yet I have not received any confirmation." He smiled and touched her cheek and Katharine felt a deep sense of longing go through her.

How could she leave this tender man, even for six weeks?

Stephen sensed there was something disturbing her. "Are you feeling all right, Katie? It's not too much for you, driving out here?"

Katharine assured him she was fine and that she was so relieved to get away from everything.

"It's really like another world," she said wistfully.

"We'll come here as often as you like. We'll call it *our* place from now on." He smiled at her and their eyes met. As they gazed at one another, Katharine felt that same pang within her. Through dinner Katharine could not find the right time to tell him about New York. Stephen was so full of the Emergency Food and Medical Bill passing, and then they discussed the concert that his brother Rick would be giving at the youth center the next Saturday afternoon. Volunteers had spent most evenings getting everything ready and Stephen said, "You'll be amazed at what the old supermarket looks like now."

"I don't know if I will ever get over my feelings for that place. . . ." Katharine wondered out loud, thinking of Jamie.

"You will. As soon as you see those kids' faces on Saturday. Thanks to you, they are going to have a chance to succeed in this world. These children can change. The center is going to give them hope—they'll be assured of our Lord's love for them." Stephen's eyes were shining. "I have even lined up someone who's going to speak to them briefly after the concert, but I'm not going to tell you who. . . ."

Katharine said excitedly, "Oh, please do tell me!"

He laughed at her eagerness. "Not on your life! I want it to be a surprise."

The waiter approached Stephen and said there was a phone call for him. He got up quickly and gave Katharine a brief kiss. "Sorry," he whispered, "I'll be back as soon as possible."

Katharine watched him as he ducked under the low doorway, leading to the foyer. He turned and smiled at her. That smile, the way he looked at her, the excitement she felt whenever she was near him—at that moment, she could give up her career if it meant having to be apart from him. But there were many questions that had to be answered.

Stephen returned in a few minutes. "See, I told you I couldn't leave you for long." He squeezed her hand and returned to eating his roast beef, the inn's specialty. Katharine wondered who had called him. Stephen sensed her curiosity. "It was Maggie. I don't know why she had to call—it could have waited until tomorrow."

He looked up and saw Katharine's troubled expression. "What's wrong?" Then, as if remembering what might be the problem—"Did Julia Simpson's garbage upset you?" Katharine nodded, then looked down at her plate. Stephen said gently, "Oh, Katie, there was absolutely nothing to that stupid gossip of hers."

Katharine picked up her fork, turning it above

her plate, as she waited for some more explanation from him. When he saw her anticipation, he said, "We haven't had a chance to talk about it because of Jamie's kidnapping." He looked directly into her eyes. "Maggie knows the British ambassador's wife and was invited to the party at the embassy by her. Julia's column was so ludicrous, I put it out of my mind."

"I wish I could have done so, Stephen, but it hurt . . ."

"Maggie is my secretary, Katharine. That's all. She's important in my life solely because she is a first-rate secretary and knows the workings of the Senate backwards. Her father having been a senator makes it everyday knowledge to her."

"But she does just so happen to be in love with you, Stephen." He laughed. "No, it's true. Perhaps you're too busy to see it, or perhaps you take her for granted, but she is in love with you."

"I have read that the best secretaries are the ones who are in love with their bosses!" Stephen said, lightheartedly, but obviously concerned about Katharine.

Katharine, fighting back her emotions said, "Your mother seems to favor her, Stephen."

"My *mother?*" Stephen laughed again. "My mother doesn't seem to favor anyone at this point except *you.*"

"Me?"

"Yes. I have received so many phone calls from her since she met you. Then when the kidnapping happened and she saw the way you handled it on the news, plus the fact that all her friends kept calling and saying how wonderful you were—well, she says she has changed her mind about the media. For her, there is at least one worthwhile person now handling the news."

Katharine sat back in her chair, completely confused. "Then why did she treat me so coldly when I was at 'Kingsridge'?"

"Katie, in spite of the fact that my mother is known prominently in certain circles, she has never yet overcome her shyness when she meets people outside of those circles. When I told her I thought she had acted very coolly to you, she told me she hadn't realized—she was as nervous as you were."

Katharine did not know whether to be convinced or not. It appeared to be such a complete change of attitude. Stephen put his hand out to her and she took it. "I love you, Katie, always remember that."

Tears stung her eyes. "I know and I love you. Stephen, there's something I have to tell you..."

Stephen interrupted. "There's something I have to tell you, but let's wait until we go out into the garden." He asked the waiter if he would bring their dessert and coffee outside, and then Stephen led Katharine out into the sparkling summer evening.

"I do believe I feel a slight nip in the air," Katharine said, relieved to think that perhaps the long humid summer was ending. Stars were beginning to come out and the moon, that Stephen had "ordered," shone through the trees—bathing the garden in a soft, romantic light. They passed a sundial while walking to the table. *Tempis fugit* was engraved on it.

Stephen remarked, "Time does indeed fly, Katharine. I want us always to value each hour, each day we have together." He kissed her tenderly, while seating her at their table.

He noticed a concerned look on her face. "Katharine, whatever is troubling you?"

His comments on valuing their time together had made the decision about New York even harder.

"Well," she said searching for the right words, "it's as they say, 'Good news and bad news.' I have been asked to go to New York for six weeks to substitute for John Webster, the anchorman there. It could lead to a permanent position..."

Stephen seemed overwhelmed. "I see." He thought for a moment. "Well, of course, I'm very happy for you. It's what you wanted, isn't it? To anchor nationally?"

"Yes." Tears glistened in her eyes.

Stephen looked away. "I must say you have taken my breath away. I really hadn't thought about us ever being apart. I don't know whether I should tell you what I had been saving for later this evening." He looked up at the stars, deep in thought. "I don't want to stand in your way, Katharine. I love you too much for that. I know what this would mean to you. You're so deserving of it. You're . . ." He let out a long sigh.

Katharine touched his sleeve, the nearness of him making her want to say she didn't want to go . . . she wouldn't leave him. Stephen took her hand and kissed it gently. She could see he was turning something over and over in his mind.

"Perhaps what I was going to ask you is unfair to you, right now. This offer of New York might only come once in a lifetime and I wouldn't want you to ever regret not going."

Katharine asked him, "What was it you were going to say before I told you about New York?"

The waiter came with their dessert and coffee and Katharine felt as if he would never leave.

After he was gone, Stephen said, softly, "I was going to ask you to marry me, Katharine."

"Oh, Stephen," she whispered, feeling her heart skip a beat. She loved this man so much.

She had prayed that if it were God's will they would marry. Now, here was Stephen offering her a life with him...and yet she hesitated.

"I want to be your wife, but I don't know...I don't know what to say. If I took the New York position, I could never be a real wife to you. It would mean being separated so much. You deserve more than just a 'weekend wife.' "

"Isn't our love great enough that we could work out any problems that might come between us?"

Katharine held his hand tightly and closed her eyes.

"I don't know, Stephen." She envisioned what her life would be like in New York. It would mean practically total commitment to her work. She thought of the prestige of anchoring nationally. She would have the satisfaction of having accomplished what she had set out to do, but it would be empty without Stephen by her side.

"God has a way of altering our plans," Katharine's father's words came back to her. She remembered him telling her years before, "Always be faithful to His will, Katie. Learn to be adaptable, to adjust to life." She knew he had realized that her innate will to achieve—her determination—could stand in the way of what God intended for her. "Put Him first and you will know that inner peace that the world strives for . . ."

"Stephen," she said, her voice breaking, "at the moment, I don't know what God's will is for me."

He looked at her tenderly and said, "Remember Hattie, my old governess?" Katharine nodded. "Whenever I didn't know what to do, she would tell me, 'David, the psalmist, gave us the words that will always help you to know God's will: Commit thy way unto the Lord, trust also in him and he will bring it to pass.' That's what we have got to do now, Katharine, commit everything to Him and trust Him. He will show us His sovereign will, I promise you."

In the peace of the garden, with the moonlight shining on their faces, they quietly committed their lives and love to God.

Chapter Thirteen

The line of teenagers extended around the youth center and ran like a jostling caterpillar through the parking lot. It seemed as if the whole neighborhood had turned out to hear Rick Douglass.

Katharine was delighted when she saw the transformation of the old supermarket. Its dilapidated facade had taken on a bright, gleaming look. Inside, sports equipment, tables, and chairs and an up-to-date snack bar had all been installed. Rows of chairs were set up for the concert, in front of a large stage.

"It's wonderful!" Katharine exclaimed. "I still can't believe all that has been accomplished."

"It's been a labor of love. My prayer group from the Hill has spent most of their spare time working here." Stephen put his arm through hers as they proceeded through the building. "When God gave you the inspiration for this project, He let you see your dream come true, Kate."

She kissed him. "I might have envisioned the dream, but besides sharing the inspiration, you and your friends had the muscle and the paint brushes."

They looked at each other and their smiles turned to an expression of yearning. Katharine would have to call the network soon to let them know her decision. She had slept very little, tossing and turning, trying to work out just what she should decide. Having given her problem over to God, very humanly she had taken it back again and the loneliness of the night had seemed to magnify its dimension.

From outside, Stephen and Katharine heard the squeals and screams that heralded Rick's arrival. "They didn't do that when I walked past them," Stephen said jokingly.

Rick struggled through the back door, dressed in his flashy, country clothes—followed by his band. "Well, you have to admit your senatorial navy blue suit can't compare to Rick's fancy clothes," Katharine teased.

"I should have worn my fabulous disguise," Stephen said, somewhat regretfully.

"The one you wore to the library? Your mother would faint if you wore those duds to the reception at 'Kingsridge' this evening."

They went over to Rick and Stephen introduced Katharine to him.

"Thank you so much for giving this concert. It's really going to launch the opening of the center with a 'bang'!" Katharine said. She noticed that Rick was so like his brother—especially the same disarming Douglass smile and easy manner. Both men were equally handsome, but Rick's face showed the stressful life he led.

"Katharine, I have heard so much about you. As you well know, my brother never shuts up as it is. But I agree with everything he's told me—you're as lovely as he said and it's really my pleasure to have been asked here this afternoon."

Senator Fraser joined them and introduced his wife to everyone. "The crowd is so large, we're going to need prayer just to keep them in order," he said jokingly. "Seriously, before we open the doors let's thank the Lord for this opportunity and ask Him to help us reach these kids this afternoon."

After a short prayer, the doors were flung open and the teenagers descended like locusts. At first there were a few tense moments, but, miraculously, order was quickly established as all the seats filled. Others crowded into the standing room at the back. Senator Fraser introduced Rick and his band. The first note from Rick's guitar sent a roar of approval through the large auditorium. The enthusiastic audience was captivated by him.

Rick sang and played many of his hits—to deafening applause. Then, quietly, he began to talk to them. "I'm glad you are enjoying this afternoon—I know I am. There's a young lady here whose dream made this all possible and I want her to stand. She's Katharine Hayes, from WNSC, and she believed in this project because she cared about you all. You know, when she interviewed some of you a few weeks ago you made a big impression on her. Well, that day the idea for this center was born in her heart. I want you to give her a big hand."

With tears in her eyes, Katharine stood. She realized the Lord had given her the dream and she could take none of the credit. She smiled and waved to the cheering teenagers. As she sat down Stephen took her hand.

"They love you and I'm not surprised. But not half as much as I do," he whispered, smiling at her.

"I love you, too—even though you still haven't told me who the special speaker is today."

Stephen took a quick look around the auditorium. "I guess he didn't show up. Oh, well, I'll have to substitute for him," and he pulled some notes out of his inside pocket.

Katharine laughed quietly. "It was *you* all the time!"

"I'm afraid so. You know me—can't miss an

opportunity to talk to a captive audience."

He put his arm around her shoulder and she took his hand and kissed it—her eyes revealing how pleased she was.

Rick had finished several songs, each one receiving a tremendous ovation. Then he put down his guitar and paused for a moment.

"You're a fantastic audience and I wouldn't have missed being with you for anything. I just came from California, where something incredible happened to me." The teenagers settled back in their seats, listening intently. "I guess some of you might envy me all the success I have been fortunate enough to attain, but you know, I kept feeling like a lot of you must feel—empty, wondering where my life was really going. Well, God led me to some friends who one night took me to a beach in Malibu and there, after a barbecue, they told me that that hole inside of me that seemed to be getting bigger each day— that void—could be filled with God's love. It's hard to describe, because it's all so new. I asked God's Son to come in and fill that great hole in my life and do you know? He did! He says in His Word that He will make all things new."

Katharine turned to Stephen and could see tears in his eyes. "It's what I've prayed for, Katie, for so long." She squeezed his arm, unable to say anything.

"God bless each and every one of you. Hope you'll invite me back soon." Rick waved to the crowd and when the applause died down he said, "I'm not the fancy talker my brother is. I want him to tell you more about what good things can happen in your life. Let me introduce him to you—Senator Stephen Douglass, or, as I know him, big brother Steve."

Stephen jumped up on the platform and the crowd gave him a big welcome. The brothers hugged each other and Stephen said, "You know, Rick, we don't get to see much of each other these days, but I can tell I have been blessed in having a brother like you." He grinned at the crowd. "Of course, that doesn't mean there weren't days when I would have been delighted to donate him to the Goodwill!" The teenagers laughed, nudging one another, many obviously having younger brothers and sisters.

"I'm going to make this brief, but I did just want to tell you that what happened to Rick can happen to each of you. You don't have to be famous like he is. Each one of us can know deep down inside that we are loved and accepted."

Katharine watched Stephen's face intently . . . she could see that same resolve and steadfast expression that he had revealed the night he shared his dreams and aspirations as they walked along the Potomac.

"Oh, God," she prayed silently, "show me that I'm really meant to be this remarkable man's wife. Take away any desire to go to New York—if it's not Your will."

Stephen was telling the crowd that, like Rick, he had given his life to the Lord. "One day, on a hill near my home in Virginia—I turned this life of mine over to Jesus Christ. He forgave all my sins—and forgot all my past. Knowing that He loves me, even with all my flaws, is something to this day I can't ever take for granted.

"I'll leave you with a verse from the Bible, that has come to mean a great deal to me." Momentarily he looked Katharine's way. " 'Commit your way unto the Lord; trust also in him; and he shall bring it to pass.'

"In other words, first you give your life and desires over to God, and then you trust Him. Finally in His time He will fill your life with love and blessings—showing you what's best for you."

Senator Fraser closed in prayer and afterward many of the young people stayed to talk to Rick, Stephen, Katharine, and the members of the committee—wanting to give their lives to the Lord.

●　　　●　　　●

The sweeping lawns and stately mansion made a gracious setting for Mrs. Douglass' reception at "Kingsridge." She greeted Katharine warmly and immediately took her by the arm, asking Stephen to take over the welcoming of the other guests.

"I wanted to have a word with you, Katharine. I must have seemed very uncaring the last time you were here and I apologize."

Accepting the apology lovingly, Katharine smiled and quickly changed the subject. "Thank you for giving this reception. Everyone has worked so hard to make the center's opening a success. I wish you could have seen your two sons as they spoke to the young people. They were wonderful."

"I will have to come and see it all firsthand soon," Mrs. Douglass said as they walked down the lawn to a small white gazebo. The summer house overlooked the magnificent valley, and Mrs. Douglass invited Katharine to sit with her for a few minutes.

"Katharine, I'm really very thankful that Stephen has found you. He's told me how much he loves you and that he wants to marry you." A smile broke out on her usually stern face. "You have the gifts that would make him a good wife. Then too, 'Kingsridge' would be in very capable hands, one day..."

She leaned forward and patted Katharine's hand. "Please know—I hope you'll say 'Yes.' "

Katharine was completely overwhelmed. In spite of her prior feelings about Mrs. Douglass, the Lord had answered the prayer to help her love this woman and in turn it had been reciprocated.

"Thank you, Mrs. Douglass. I'm really praying about it. I love Stephen so very much . . ."

Stephen came running up to the gazebo. "There you are. Some guests are arriving that I want you to meet, Mother. I'm sure Katharine would want to see them, too."

They all walked toward the mansion and there Katharine's family was waiting on the veranda. It was a complete surprise to her.

"Thought it would be a good opportunity for the families to meet," Stephen whispered to her. Katharine held his arm and said a quiet "Thank you."

Jamie and Beth came running down the steps to meet Katharine and Stephen. Immediately after hugs and kisses, they started asking Stephen questions about "Kingsridge," and where were the horses, and could they go riding?

Ellen tried to stop them from pestering but Stephen insisted that he would find someone to take the children to see the horses. Rick volunteered and Jamie and Beth excitedly went off with him, questioning him all the way.

Katharine's mother and father, with Ellen and Jim joining them, soon became caught up in conversation with Mrs. Douglass as they sat on the veranda.

"Could we slip away for a few minutes?" Katharine asked Stephen. "There's something I want to tell you."

He looked down at her, searching those compellingly lovely blue eyes. For a moment, Stephen stood transfixed by her beauty. Without saying a word, he took her hand and led her into the house, through the lofty, imposing hall, exiting through the back door. Katharine felt a special sense of excitement go through her as she realized he was heading to the hill where he had taken her on her first visit to "Kingsridge."

"We'll drive—those shoes you're wearing would never make it." Stephen kissed her and held her close for a few seconds, then he opened the door for her.

The drive only took a few minutes and Katharine felt her heart beating faster and faster. There was so much she wanted to say to him and she wondered where she was going to begin. The car reached the summit and quickly they both got out and walked to the ridge. A few lights twinkled in the late summer evening, the valley seeming to welcome them.

They stood, locked in each other's arms—then Stephen kissed her and Katharine felt as if all her resistance, all her questions, were melting away. Reluctantly, she pulled away from him and went over to sit under a tall, proud oak tree—reaching out her hand to him. Stephen took it and sat down beside her, his arm around her shoulders.

"What is it you want to tell me, Katie?"

She hesitated—knowing that what she was about to say would alter the course of her whole life. "Stephen, this afternoon while we were at the center, I asked God to take away any desire from my heart concerning New York—if it were His will."

"And did He?"

She turned to look at Stephen, a smile lighting up her face. "Yes. I knew without any doubt whatsoever that I should remain in Washington. I would be so lonely without you, Stephen. I couldn't bear to think of us being apart..."

He said quietly, "But, Katie, it's something you've worked for and dreamed of for so long. I want you to be absolutely sure."

"Does that mean you have had second thoughts about our getting married?" Katharine said, somewhat nervously.

He laughed. "Second thoughts? Yes, I have had second, third, and fourth thoughts, and do you know what?"

"What?"

"All my thoughts are the same—I love and adore you, Katie, and more than anything in this world I want you to be my wife. But I would never, ever want you to think I stood in the way of your career. On the other hand, if you went to New York I would feel as if part of me were missing—knowing you were so far away. But I would sooner spend the rest of my life with you—even if it meant times of separation—than with any other woman in this world."

"That's how I feel about you, darling Stephen. But being close to you means everything to me. I just can't ever leave you."

Stephen turned her face toward him. "Does this mean you'll marry me?"

"Yes." It was barely a whisper, but Katharine felt as if the entire valley must have heard. The intensity of her feelings made her whole being want to tell the world that the man beside her was going to be her husband.

Their arms were around each other and tears glistened in Katharine's eyes. "God has brought us together, Stephen, and I always want to make you happy."

"Oh, Katharine!" His face against hers pulsed with an eagerness that made her deeply aware of the depth of his love. Stephen looked down at the valley, watching the ever-changing scene.

"Every important decision I have made in my life has been made here. My decision for the Lord, what college I would go to, if I should run for the Senate and now . . ." He held her close to him. "Oh, Katie, we'll accomplish so much together. You'll see. With you by my side there is a world out there that needs our help, and in whatever way God calls us, we'll become involved."

"As a senator's wife, I know I'll feel very much a participant," Katharine said, feeling excited as she thought of all that there would be to achieve.

"Yes, oh, yes. Politics is one of the jobs in which a wife—especially one like you—can make such a difference."

"Whatever talents He has given me can be used in our marriage. I know I'll be kept busy. Right now, all I can think of is being with you. Living in your house . . ."

"*Our* house," Stephen corrected her with a smile.

"*Our* house. Oh, yes. That sounds wonderful. I won't have to lie awake in bed anymore, thinking of you living three streets away." Katharine laughed out loud. "Oh, I can't believe this is really happening!"

"It is—love is really ours, darling Katie." He kissed her once again, their desire and love for each other heightening the joy they felt.

Stephen helped Katharine to her feet and whispered, "Let's go and tell our families. . ."

As they were walking back to the station wagon, hand in hand, he stopped abruptly and looked down at Katharine.

"One question—you'll go on working at WNSC, at least for a while?"

Katharine nodded.

"Well," Stephen said thoughtfully. "Could I make a request?"

"Of course. Anything."

"Could you ask them for a transfer to the six o'clock news? Your hours are killing me!"

Katharine laughed, burying her face in his chest. "I'll put in my request on Monday." Then gazing up at him she whispered, jokingly, "I really haven't sacrificed anything, you know—giving up the possibility of being a network anchorwoman. After all, being married to you, one day I just might become First Lady!"

Stephen laughed with her, then a serious expression came into his eyes.

"Who knows, sweet Kate, who knows?"